RANDOM ACTS
OF
HATRED

RANDOM

ACTS

OF

HATRED

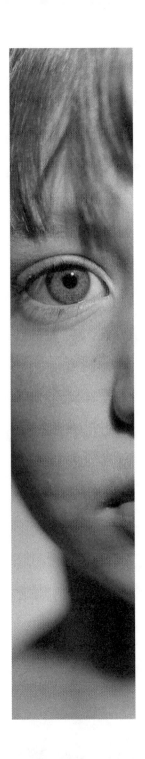

GEORGE K. ILSELY

ARSENAL
PULP PRESS
Vancouver

ARSENAL PULP PRESS
103 – 1014 Homer Street
Vancouver, B.C.
Canada V6B 2W9
arsenalpulp.com

The publisher gratefully acknowledges the support of the Canada Council for the Arts and the
British Columbia Arts Council for its publishing program, and the Government of Canada
through the Book Publishing Industry Development Program for its publishing activities.

Design by Solo
Cover photography by Rosalee Hiebert

Printed and bound in Canada

This is a work of fiction. Any resemblance of characters to persons
either living or deceased is purely coincidental.

National Library of Canada
Cataloguing in Publication Data

Ilsley, George K., 1958–
 Random acts of hatred / George K. Ilsley.

     ISBN 1-55152-152-0
     I. Title.
PS567.L84R36 2003   C813'.6   C2003-911202-0

*Dedicated to the
enlightenment of all
sentient beings*

CONTENTS

Our Boy   9

The Relative Bargain   31

When Parrots Bark   41

The Boy Who Stopped   47

The Brochure   63

Against Nature   69

The Compassion Club   85

Christmas in Kathmandu   103

The Big Red Picture   109

Random Acts of Hatred   123

Acting Innocent   127

Talismen   159

Acknowledgments   171

OUR BOY

The boy who was Christian during puberty was Christian during puberty with his mother.

She had company for church and he had a hopeful, tenacious innocence. She never seemed so obviously proud of him, not of his report cards or general helpfulness, as she did those spring mornings driving their push-button automatic to morning mass at the Anglican church in Auburn. Pleasing his mother still made him happy, but at the same time he knew he was on the verge of finding such easy sentiment complicated.

His mother's cologne overwhelmed the air in the car, the windows rolled shut against the pig barns – to the boy, a different, but equal, stench – and to protect her hat, a small green peculiar confection fringed with a vestigial veil. Her fresh drugstore-perm seemed a precarious perch, yet her hats never budged. Hats made her careful. She smiled without moving.

On the dash the gear buttons, like radio stations, were selected with the push of a single pointed finger: Reverse, Park, Drive. The boy thought these push-button gears were neat. He grew to realize men were offended by the simple design. Men, apparently, need to handle a stick to feel involved in the driving experience.

Gripping the steering wheel at ten and two o'clock, his mother's thick garden-roughened hands strained the seams of her beige gloves. Old Mrs Cunningham, she informed him without turning her head, had called in a snit about all the church busybodies with nothing better to do than gossip. "What do they say about me," his mother wondered and paused, as if he might answer. "Well, never mind. Let them beat their gums. I don't care."

The Valley was fast becoming a hive of strip malls joined by new roads. The small Anglican church, in a community that did not merit an exit when they put through the highway, radiated an aura strong enough to attract a commuter congregation.

The church's old brick walls were held together – supposedly – by mortar made from the shells of mussels collected by fugitives fleeing the ethnic cleansing which swept the Bay of Fundy more than two centuries ago (now known as The Expulsion of the Acadians, and less well known as *Le Grand Dérangement*). A band of refugees tried to overwinter along the shore, braving the elements, but winter knows no mercy. Spring killed off the few who lived to feel the touch of its treacherous warmth.

Now, where they died, is a small mortared-stone monument, the French Cross.

And in the Valley, nestled in the bosom of the Land of Evangeline, the small, white, Anglican church stood isolated by its own parking lot, slightly shabby and fabulously quaint.

For the boy, the stained glass crucifixion tableau fed on that refugee midden, nourished in spirit by the heat of the bodies and the blood of men who communed with the hard-shelled misery of mussels until they expired in a heap.

And there was something about the boy who was christian during puberty who savoured the depictions of a lanky, blond Christ, loin-clothed and enduring his torment. The boy tingled at the very core of his being. Christ was also a son of god who came to be recognized. This was to be, above all, an offering of vindication.

The blossoming of his christianity coincided with an acute awareness of virginity. His virginity. He wondered if there could be another virgin birth. A son of god born of a virgin. Born of him.

He remained a virgin throughout confirmation classes. His nascent faith rested on the theory that confirmation was the key. Any reception problems he was experiencing with his channel to god would be cleaned up by confirmation. Our boy was keen for a good clear signal. *Cataclysm*, he'd called the text, an honest mistake. Reverend Clapham corrected him with a thin smile. *Not cataclysm. Catechism.*

He was a virgin when Reverend Clapham took him aside and told him that "to be with another boy was wrong."

Our boy was shocked. He didn't know what "to be" with another boy really meant. But he knew the minister meant *something*, and he now felt much more definite about *something* inside him being wrong.

He just wondered how obviously wrong. He wondered if the minister warned all the boys at cataclysm. There was no way to find out. He couldn't ask.

Maybe it was just the minister. Maybe he had special training, and could see into the secret heart of a polite, bookish, sensitive boy who attended church with his mother.

The minister was the first to mention what our boy could not have explained. It was a secret to him, too, his feelings about boys, whatever they were – most often fear, and a strange hope, and overwhelming envy, but also a kind of hollow longing branching out into a dreamy fanciful wistfulness he couldn't have begun to describe.

"Such feelings will never bear fruit," the minister said, as if he could read the boy's dread. *Fruit* indeed was one word the boy was called. He was different, anyone could see that. But how? Besides being clean and smart – how was he different, and how much could people see who knew what to look for?

He never pondered anything a minister said as much as that warning not to be with another boy. A warning about *something*. He thought about what *something* could be. To be or not to be – that was Shakespeare, but to be with a boy, or not to be with a boy – was that Shakespeare?

There were too many questions, each one fed by the lack of a good answer.

The Right Reverend Clapham, High Anglican, was soft-spoken and pudgy. A roll of flesh bulged, glistening, over his damp collar. His congregation of middle-aged housewives found the idea of tea with the minister ("right chatty he is, a bit of an old hen, isn't he, never stops clucking") both flattering and tedious.

Long afternoons wrestling with coffee cake and conversation the Reverend logged in his date book as "Community Outreach." Despite trafficking in gossip like it was the opiate of the masses, soft tones evoking concern, but never a whisper of malice, Reverend Clapham remained steadfastly unaware that his own son was the drug dealer in junior high.

At least, that was his son's reputation. (Another rumour was that corn silk, and the dried threads from banana skins, were extremely potent if smoked. You could hallucinate.)

Greg Clapham, the minister's son, was legendary. He instigated a "classic prank," he called it, to leave "pasture pies" in a paper sack on the principal's doorstep. "In India cows are holy," Greg advised, "so this is a sacred rite." He lit the bag afire, rang the doorbell, and scrambled.

One of his gang of copycats, having lost the element of surprise, was nabbed in an ambush. Refusing to squeal on the others, he was suspended for a week, and his parents beat the crap out of him.

Greg Clapham bragged of his escapades, like when old "Cuntingham" had phoned Greg's mother to report that with all her own lights off she was able to see into her neighbour's yard and, right in back, "Greg's in the bush with that Hawkins girl. You know the one. Just thought you should know."

Jennifer Hawkins. At that time young Greg was wildly mad about Jenny and her moist brown eyes, and was so close to having her right there when his mother started yelling. Jennifer buttoned up fast, acting all cool and normal in a stunning transition, while he was still thick and dumb with lust. The soft smell of her slid off his fingers as Jennifer morphed back to sweet innocence, calling out, *Be right there, Missus Clapham.* Her effortless pleasant deceit overlapped with the images seared into Greg: her face looking possessed, eyes bottomless with longing. She looked – horny. *She's a slut*, he realized. He did not want a girl another guy could have. He felt disgusted, but still – she was good for a bone. Sluts are also good for proving that chicks *are* sluts. Greg was furious at the disruption. He was already counting on bragging about this to the copycats. For revenge, Greg thought of Krazy Gluing the locks on the neighbours' car, but that cost money. Instead he just drained a little brake fluid. Old Mr Cunningham, on his way uptown for the mail, rolled down the driveway pumping and pumping the brakes, too flustered to remember to steer. He rolled straight across the road and into the ditch on the other side, breaking his dentures when the steering wheel bounced up and smacked him in the face. Greg felt a twinge in his gut when he saw the old man after the accident, lips swollen and sunken, stitches puckering the bruised flesh. That old bastard shouldn't even be driving anymore, Greg realized, and then felt better. He's a menace. And that mean dried-up old sow should keep her snout in her own trough.

People who don't mind their own damn business just get what they deserve.

Everyone knew ministers' kids were the worst. Ministers' daughters were major sluts in town after town, and the sons drug dealers when there weren't even drugs. In every new parish, people said, *What little angels*, and expected the worst.

Knowing nods, lips pursed: *The cobbler's children always go barefoot.*

The boy who was christian during puberty knew cobblers only from fairy tales.

It all made our boy seriously wonder what anyone knew about him, and what they knew, really, about anything.

14

The boy who was christian during puberty stopped fantasizing about any kind of virgin birth after Greg Clapham, the minister's son, was done with him. In the woods behind Cottage Street our boy froze, eyes gleaming moistly, caught in the glare of Greg's physical, compelling presence. The leer was a promise, threatening and inevitable. They acted out the roles with a timeless, furtive choreography. "Come here," Greg said. "Do it." Our boy's sense of divinity was overwhelmed. He too was stunned by beauty.

The second time Greg hit him, a mirrorball reeled around the edges of a swelling, lopsided darkness. His tears choked him.

"Do it." Greg's words were thick, his sullen features an admixture of fascination and a deep, desperate, disgust.

II. IN LOVE FOR THE FIRST TIME

The boy who was in love for the first time had been out all night, camping. With a tent. Laughter came so easily they were practically hysterical just at the idea of camping – with a tent. They attended the ballet while camping, for crying out loud. If they were not already self-aware, over-achieving little faggots – what were they?

Our boy first noticed the other boy at Rumours, the one mostly gay bar in the provincial capital. The boys eyed each other shyly for several nights without being obvious. Then their eyes locked and held and after a moment of stunned silence, they finally chatted.

Our boy had mentioned working for the season at a tourist-trap waterfront restaurant. The other boy dropped by. They traded phone numbers, and felt the onset of being adult, which manifests itself, apparently, as lightheadedness, and a tight aching thud in the chest.

The next day they talked for over an hour on the phone. The other boy suggested camping. And the ballet. "Ballet and camping," our boy mused out loud. "Will that be enough for an evening?" They burst out laughing. It was comforting to know they could mock things down to scale. *Camping – with a tent.*

Alone in his summer sublet, the door closed, our boy grimaced into sudden tears. *How could HE be interested in ME?* The sheer weight of it all was terrifying, being too big to trust.

He shrugged off his outburst, each T-shirt shoulder rising in turn, like crossing the street, left then right then left again. Sniffle. Done.

Our boy had a teeny-tiny flair for the dramatic.

His innocence was honest, yet arrogant. When you're that young – nineteen, twenty – you can be so totally sure, yet not believe a thing, and see no contradiction.

He remembered the other boy's eyes, a dark captivating depth like shaded green pools. His wave of distress subsided, and he felt himself growing into his new dimensions, flooded with an overwhelming warmth and certainty, like an emotional wet dream.

It was overwhelming, and it was impossible.

He expected to wake up, and feel cheated, and worst of all, mad. At himself. One could hope, yes, but reaching so high was foolish.

The boy who was in love for the first time was in love with a young god. Handsome. Athletic. Captain of the swim team. Member of the student council. Popular, and friendly. Shaggy mane of blond hair, streaked from sun and chlorine and, as it turned out, lemon juice and Sun-In.

Swimgod was sexy.

RANDOM ACTS OF HATRED

Swimgod was everything our boy was not.

They weren't to be alone at the campground, our two boys in a four-man tent. Swimgod brought two friends he introduced as the "selection committee." Our boy was startled by their appearance, and crushed by the introduction. *Selection committee?* He felt himself shrinking.

The selection committee was a guy and a girl, a couple. Nice people. Swimmers, the three of them friends for years. They even dressed alike, casual jock uniforms of jeans and t-shirts, k-Way windbreakers and sweatshirts branded by universities. Our boy was outfitted in thrift-store eccentric: Glen tartan pants, hound's-tooth vest, and a purple shirt many would consider gaudy. His dark herringbone tweed jacket was too large. People stared. His quirky personality was engaging, even charming (he was almost sure of that), but his best features were elusive, if not altogether ambiguous.

When nervous, our boy tended to be silent, or garrulous. With Swimgod's friends he became monosyllabic. (The selection committee reported him as "quiet.")

At the campground, the selection committee casually planned the sleeping arrangements with a zealous attention to detail. Some sleeping bags zipped together, but one did not, so they needed to know the plan. Our boy was obviously a last-minute addition. A complication. The girl suggested that our boy, who had supplied none of the equipment, use the single bag. The other three could share one giant zipped-together bag.

One of these things is not like the others. A *Sesame Street* song played in his head.

One of these things doesn't belong.

It made no sense, but what could he say? He showed his teeth and grunted compliance.

Our boy and Swimgod drove into town to see the ballet – as fluttery and glacial as on television, but much noisier. Dancers sound heavier than they look. The thinnest leaping gazelle in a tutu landed with lead in her slippers. Dust jolted from the floorboards and rose in the air.

Swimgod watched the performance entranced. Our boy kept an eye on Swimgod. The line of his thighs swept up like an invitation. Sitting next to this young man in Convocation Hall, surrounded by the dusty thuds and shuffles of the ballet, he felt a rush both of identity and dislocation: *Is this really me? Am I really on this date?*

After the ballet they walked a bit but there were couples everywhere, strolling innocently arm in arm. Our boys did not dare hold hands, even in the midst of this post-ballet crowd. Unable even to voice their frustration, they decided to go back to the campground.

In the car, our boy was stewing so he thought he'd ask. "Why did you bring them?"

"Who?"

"Who else? Your friends. The *selection committee.*" Our boy instantly regretted his nagging tone. He sounded like his mother.

Swimgod said, "I dunno," in a flat way.

Silence loomed in the car. "What did you think of the ballet?" our boy finally asked.

"Felt like I was on a trip."

"A trip."

"Yeah. They took me somewhere."

"Where?"

"I dunno. Somewhere else."

Back at the campground, Swimgod's friends waved them over to the picnic table for a beer. The swimmers traded war stories. One particular coach they loved to hate. He tied his swimmers to the end of the pool with a length of rubber tubing. "There was no incentive at all," Swimgod laughed. "You'd be flailing away like a maniac, and if you ever made it to the far wall, you just got a shorter piece of rubber."

"And he was big on pantyhose." The swimmers chuckled. "Loved pantyhose."

Our boy was confused.

"You see, when you shave down to qualify, you couldn't shave again in couple of weeks. Well, you could, but it wouldn't have any effect." Swimgod drained his beer. "So in the meantime he'd make you train wearing pantyhose, to replace the drag of the hair."

"The drag of the hair!" Our boy laughed out loud, then stopped. He was still confused.

Swimgod squeezed his knee under the picnic table. "Let's go for a walk."

He put his hand over Swimgod's. "Okay," he said. The beer had fuelled a reckless, brazen impulse. He stood up and quickly turned away.

"In the dark?" asked the girl, incredulous.

"You get used to it," Swimgod said. "The moon's out."

Darkness quickly surrounded them with a cocoon of privacy.

Far from the others, our boy stopped to repeat some revelation to his new friend, seeking to discuss a mediocre aspect of the ballet's staging – and there, glowing in the moonlight, was this divine creature.

Our Boy

"You know why I brought them?" Swimgod was close enough to feel his warm breath, tangy and richly sweet, like the aftertaste of communion. His eyes glittered, dark and deep.

"Why?"

Swimgod licked his lips. "For protection, I suppose."

"From what?"

Swimgod shifted his weight and shrugged, then relaxed his shoulders and displayed a gloriously wicked grin. "From myself?" The grin faltered.

The boy couldn't help himself. The bottom fell out of his heart and overwhelmingly inclined, he accepted the abyss. Spread his arms out and leaned forward. His face met the boy's face, their warm breath collided and their lips met. Their hands felt and felt, and held on.

The two boys paused to take a breath and looked at each other, very serious, then necked like fools in the perfect darkness, and the boys who fell in love for the first time did just that.

In his arms he held the boy who was everything he was not and thought, *This is different.*

In the mirror of the kiss, each boy saw a new face. His self-image was shattered and reborn, and he became, for a long moment, undefined and unknowable. In that space, in that moment, something happened. Their future, their relationship, their first kiss, everything.

Back at the tent, our boy headed for bed while Swimgod went for a shower, claiming he'd "been outta the water too long."

The selection committee was in the middle of the tent. The

single bag for our boy was on one side. Next to him in the giant zipped-together bag was the girl, then the guy. Against the far wall of the tent space was left for Swimgod.

When Swimgod tried to crawl into the tent, feet blocked the entrance. "Hey, it's a herd of baby cows in here," he said. He located our boy and groped among the other legs. "C'mon, you guys. Move over."

There was no right way to say, *No, the place we made for you to sleep is way over there.* The selection committee slid over like sidewinders, and Swimgod crawled in next to our boy. They turned towards each other, held hands, and waited.

Much of the night was spent touching faces with fingertips and lips. Kisses now tasted like sweet mint. A gentle, quiet necking transformed the night into an eternity.

The boy who was in love was delirious. Tired and baffled, too. How could someone like this boy, who was everything he was not, be interested in him? "You're so smooth," Swimgod whispered. "Like silk." Swimgod was definitely a breaststroker. Our boy was surprised by the hair on his broad chest. "From shaving," Swimgod whispered. "Comes back thicker." Swimgod slid his hand down our boy's torso. "Nice."

Our boy filled with a sudden, solid conviction that attraction was a power that drew from many different directions. The other boy's erection was aligned to his own, broadcasting confirmation with every echoing pulse. The two of them were right there, the two boys holding each other, and necking, but their journeys were different. Overlapping, but different.

It was not pure bliss, this connection. There was pain as well, and joy and panic. It wasn't until he experienced each succeeding wave so keenly that our boy began to know what love meant. He ached at separation and blossomed with adoration. He was driven mad by obsession, and drank deeply of the rewards of misery. In a flash, he understood Shakespeare, and that is when he realized this was it, this is really what it means, to be in love.

To be in love with Swimgod.

22 Our boy's mother knew something had happened, and she wondered what. He wasn't the same. She couldn't remember the last time she felt she knew her son. He never stayed home, much less went to church. Of course, neither did she anymore since Mrs Cunningham died and she hated going alone.

She sat down to watch her show, and the cat jumped in her lap. The show's matriarch, "Rachel," was going blind again, which was saddening, again.

Her own son talked of buying a motorcycle and going to Mexico, which seized her in the grip of a fear so primal and nameless it could only mean some disaster worse than death. He was back at school, but still made trips to the city. And he had that friend, they were two peas in a pod. Her son was never one to be interested in pals or travel. He was a bookworm! Now he wanted to leave, and he had his buddy, but never talked about him. Clammed up even if she asked the most innocent thing.

He had secrets, it seemed, and she wondered about that.

She felt she was snooping but did it anyway. She leafed through a dog-eared paperback the boys were highlighting and handing back and forth.

Walt Whitman. "You shall scatter with lavish hand," she read marked in green. And in fluorescent orange, "The limber motion of brawny young arms and hips in easy costumes." She skipped to another place. Capitalized with pen and underlined she read, "The Moisture of the Right Man," and "The Fruits of the Gushing Showers." Right. She put the book down quickly. *Leaves of Grass.* She knew what this was. Some sort of psychedelic drug thing. A kind of rebellion, probably, harmless enough if confined to books.

She tried to keep a tight lid on worrying. But her suspicions were right there, feeding on scraps, chewing away at the edges of denial like scavengers fighting for a real meal. Without ever making the decision, she avoided naming her fear and nourishing it into voracious life.

So she hadn't meant to ask. She was napping with the cat. Her son arrived home, bouncing off the walls, whistling and full of himself. He'd been swimming, he said. *Swimming? He never went swimming.* Glowing, giggly, his mood impossibly buoyant – was he on drugs?

Startled from cover, the fear which dare not speak its name found voice.

"You and that guy, you're not just friends, are you?" She was blunt, almost coy. Her confidence flowed from the percolating comforts of a dream of her son in the garden, where they watched the rain and felt happy.

Not just friends? The boy blinked. What to do with her? He could try telling the truth. She was asking after all. Maybe she really wanted to know. *You and that guy?* He picked up the cat before he answered.

"We're lovers," he said, nuzzling the cat.

"What do you do?"

"Do?"

"With each other."

The boy stroked the cat's face with his finger, still processing the calm reaction to the news that he was gay.

"I mean," his mother said, "who is the man, and who is the woman?"

Now he was stunned. "It's . . . it's not like that."

"Well then," she said, starting to sound peeved. "What is it like?"

What could he say? Such questions were clichés, weren't they? But here was his mother on the righteous, wounded edge of angry, asking, *Who is the man and who is the woman?*

"It's private," he said, instead of saying nothing. "That's what it's like."

The cat squirmed and he let her down.

"Do you take drugs and put on ladies' clothes?"

Laughter burst past before his face could hold it. It was a mistake trying to be honest. Her genial interest had not been genuine: it was a kind of weapon, one she rarely used. He usually treated her as a "mind field," to be passed through carefully along familiar trails. Any misstep – such as laughing – could trigger an outburst. Her features turned ugly. Curiosity flipped into repulsion.

"It has to stop right now," his mother declared. "And I mean right now."

"Nothing is going to stop," he replied with equal certainty, surprised at his own boldness.

"Your father won't stand for it."

"It's none of his business."

"Oh that's where you're wrong, young man. You think you're so smart but sometimes you don't know a blessed thing." His mother bristled. "You don't know whose business this is. This is everybody's business. And if you want everybody whispering and laughing behind my back, you just keep it up."

The boy was to hear more clichés that day.

His father came home and the storm brewed and built and broke and judgment hailed down from on high. *It's just not right, it's unnatural, it's a sin.* And the final decree, *Not while living under my roof you don't.*

"Why is it wrong?" he asked. His father refused to talk about it.

The boy's face contorted into a mirror of outrage. "It doesn't matter any more what you say. Don't you get it? Don't you get it?" He sounded shrill and hated himself for that. He was acting just like his father – unyielding, vindictive, and rigid – and he hated himself for that too.

And so our boy was kicked out by his parents and told not to come back – until he changed.

If that's how the cards were dealt, he'd play them as they lay. His father wouldn't even notice, but could his mother live without him?

They could kick him out, sure, but he knew his mother. Time was on his side.

And he found easy refuge.

When our boy was kicked out for being in love, Swimgod and his parents took him in – for much the same reason.

Swimgod had parents who were a whole different story. They were ordinary enough. He worked in the bottling plant at the brewery, and drank the company brands like he lived on the royalties. She was a chain-smoking housewife who bingo'd twice a week.

They weren't at all pleased to learn their youngest was gay. He had seemed, if anything, blessed; now they worried he'd lead a miserable life, hiding in fear. But they listened to what he had to say, determined to embrace his future.

Easy-going parents typically exert clear boundaries. At that time and place, these parents seemed limitless: if you had to drink beer and smoke joints, it was better to do that in the basement. The rec room was safer than the great unknown, and supervision, though not stifling, was present. Girls could hang out and be cuddled and semi-publically heavy-petted, but were not to sleep over.

These rules had been drafted in response to the perambulations of Swimgod's older brothers. Their youngest son's friend – our boy – appeared out of the blue, and moved right in.

Our son's boyfriend did not register as a concept. By default, he became the new best friend. Even though Swimgod had clearly explained, the parents were slow to absorb the information. *Our son's boyfriend?* The boys had stumbled upon a bit of resilient denial, a heterosexist bias which, ironically, gave them their freedom.

Our boys found the gay loophole.

They both slept in Swimgod's bedroom, cuddled together talking about today and tomorrow. Their love was invisible in the way that air is invisible: everyone wallows in it, but it is not usually remarked upon. In another seeming contradiction, a denial of denial, Swimgod was told not to have sex in the house.

Conscientiously rumpling both bunk beds, the boys did not sleep separated. The bottom bunk wobbled less when they made out.

The parents had reason to be puzzled. Our boy wasn't like

Swimgod's sporty friends. And Swimgod's parents had never seen their son so prone to loll around with his nose in a book. And argue – the two of them could talk the mouth right off the harbour.

And another part of this whole other story was, our boy had a crush on the parents who offered unconditional love at just the right time. But he didn't treat them very well.

This perfectly ordinary couple, in a display of natural generosity, opened up their home to a young stranger sleeping with their youngest son. Swimgod's parents were pioneers in the new flexibility, straining and stretching the boundaries of family, because their son was in love. Their gay son-in-law sprang up overnight like a new kind of mushroom, and didn't even realize he could have treated his instant in-laws better, much better, with the unconditional respect they deserved, until years later and they were gone. One from an accident, the other cancer.

Our boy, who was christian during puberty, and who fell in love and was kicked out and told never to return until he changed, and who found easy refuge, counted the days until his mother called. A couple of warm weeks passed with the languid fluidity and buried tensions of a honeymoon. The boys made daily trips to Lake Banook while the weather held, falling into a routine – a short swim, an exquisitely risky make-out session in the car, another dip in a lake so they wouldn't reek when they got back to the house.

Swimgod's mother intercepted them at the fridge. "Your mother phoned."

"Oh," he said. "Okay."

"Aren't you going to phone her?"

"Yeah."

"So phone her."

"Okay."

"So, phone her now." The same bluntness our boy enjoyed from his friend's mother he would have resented at home. It amused him to release her from strict judgment. She pointed to the phone as she left the kitchen, waving her cigarette at her son. "Weren't you in the lake? Go take a shower!"

"Oh, hi dear," our boy's mother said. "I just wanted you to know – I'm making macaroni and cheese. With real cheese. Are your clothes dirty? Bring some laundry." Seventeen days was longer than she'd gone without talking to him since before he was born. "Of course," she said, "you're welcome to stay the night." Her casual tone implied nothing beyond the normal undercurrents of motherly anxiety, yet the need for such diplomatic overtures had never before been entertained.

Our boy said, "Maybe next week."

His laundry was already clean.

And so the boy in love became more and more like the boy he was not. They were both young, their convictions absolute and fragile, their passions consistently stormy. Everything got swept up into that vortex. All of life was volatile.

(As bitterness is an acquired taste, leave it to flavour a more sharply sardonic fairy tale, such as The Boy Who Was a Jealous God, or, The Boy Who Could Not Keep His Cock In His Pants.)

After the inevitable series of break-ups and getting back to-gether, and the almost equally inevitable move to Toronto, our boy became everything he was truly meant to be.

He became himself.

And we – all of us – held him up to the mirror.

THE RELATIVE BARGAIN

The blindfolded boy kneels on the burgundy yak wool area rug in the living room. Naked, except for a black jockstrap.

Curt wants to remember *exactly* how he manoeuvred the boy into nothing but a jockstrap and convinced him to kneel blindfolded in the middle of the living room. The pitcher of screwdrivers, of course, was instrumental. It always is. Curt makes wicked screwdrivers, heavy on the vodka, with extra lemon juice and sugar. Lots of sugar, that's the secret. Kids like their booze sweet, helps it slip down faster. Curt just keeps pouring and making promises, hinting at promotions, raises, trips to Europe.

Interviewing new staff for the store is a thrill and a challenge. Like fishing, the trick is finding the right bait.

So what was on the hook which so snagged this boy he agreed to parade around in a black jockstrap? Jockstraps in seven colours are part of the merchandise available in Curt's trendy retail outlet, Emporium. Emporium also sells snug brightly coloured singlets, ribbed T-shirts with zippers, baggy shorts in crazy patterns, Dr Seuss hats, inlaid wooden boxes, brass Hindu deities, condoms, lube, incense, and lots of glossy cards with photos of buff artsy nudes.

The boy, Devon, had inquired about the HELP WANTED sign in the store. Curt puts out the sign whenever he's in a certain restless mood. Saint James the Martyr, the one long-term employee at Emporium, rolls his eyes and mutters, *There isn't a* doubt *on Mars that man needs all the help he can* get.

Curt looked the young applicant over, sizing up how badly the kid needed a job, and grunted, "Too busy, come back another time." After Devon turned away dejected, Curt suggested, as a reluctant afterthought, an "informal interview" later at his apartment. "We could have a drink," Curt glanced at his watch, distracted, "and discuss your prospects."

Devon probably secretly dreams of becoming a model, that's why he agreed to be conned into wearing only a jockstrap. *Typical teenager*, Curt smiles knowingly. *Hasn't a clue. Doesn't really know how gorgeous he is.*

In other words, easy to exploit.

Curt travels far afield in search of the relative bargain. In the lap of luxury on Thai Air he flies across the Pacific Ocean to locate cheap skilled labour. He sources merchandise in Thailand, Indonesia, and Hong Kong, but his preferred Asian destination is Sri Lanka. Jobbers in Sri Lanka are keen to knock off clothing designs cheaply from a sample or even from a photo in a British fashion magazine. Jockstraps in seven colours and three sizes are available at a stunningly low cost. In Sri Lanka, Curt purchases aromatic sandalwood boxes and incense by the case, and little brass incense burners, and long wooden incense holders patterned with mother of pearl.

In Sri Lanka, he buys blowjobs from dark-skinned Caucasian boys with the tight, curvy bodies of gymnasts. *Cock-asians*, Curt calls them. *They're so handsome it hurts. And best of all – blowjobs in Canada cost a hundred times more!* Scoring a bargain is the best aphrodisiac.

In Sri Lanka, one can often arrange extra intense blowjobs, mind-blowing blowjobs, in exchange for comments on the youth's exceptional beauty (which is not to be underestimated – competition is fierce) and emphatic (if vague) promises about arranging for a job in Canada. A job offer in mythical Canada would be the best kind of karma, a gift from the all-powerful immigration gods, deities the youth has prayed to on his knees. "They would *love you* at the store," Curt says, stroking from the lad's head to his shoulders. "You'd be *so good* for business."

Two hundred whole rupees an hour, every hour. Today's anonymous dark-skinned *cock-asian* with a sturdy neck and perfect gleaming teeth reels under the immense weight of the imagined lifestyle that kind of money would afford. The youth has been known to suck off a fat hairy foreigner like Curt for way, way less. *Well, this guy is not so bad.* The Sri Lankan boy dreams of a job in Canada. *Not too demanding. Not compared to some of the Germans.* He applies himself with renewed enthusiasm, performing like his whole life depends on that one blowjob. The boy tries not to gag as Curt grabs the back of his head and neck and holds him firmly in place, shooting a foul tasting foreign load down the cock-asian's throat.

Devon was born in a small town in the Interior of British Columbia. Mountains hemmed him in on all sides and Devon felt imprisoned.

There was no wide-open horizon. He couldn't wait to leave the redneck attitudes, the drunken violence – his family a perfect microcosm of the isolated community. He couldn't wait long enough to finish high school, since it was taking, like, *forever*. Devon couldn't wait until he found something to go to. He just had to leave. He fled as so many do to the city. *Everything costs so fucking much*. He is desperate.

Looking for a job is like being in prison: When opportunity knocks it might be wearing a totally unexpected face. The unthinkable becomes desirable, or at least, expeditious.

Curt is personally offended by the concept of a minimum wage. He sincerely believes he would hire more staff at the store, providing more employment for the good of the whole of society, if only he wasn't drowning in red tape.

I think he's straight, this boy Devon. But he's new to the city and unskilled. Luckily – just like Saint James always says – jobs are as scarce as pimples in good airbrushed porno.

When Devon arrived at Curt's condo for the job interview, the pitcher of screwdrivers was mixed and waiting, like a spell ready to be cast. Curt gives Devon a tall glass and shows him around, talking about the treasures accumulated on his travels.

A draped, hanging, suggestive, ambiguous, trailing installation dominates the small foyer, the intersection of kitchen, living room and hall. A snake's skeleton materializes into focus, dozens of ribs plated in silver, some gold. Wing-like attachments to the spine are inlaid with semi-precious stones and asymmetrical shell designs. Covering the snake's skull is a leather hood with silver outlining details.

"It's a python," Curt says. "An Indian python. In the jungle these suckers are good in the trees. They catch monkeys, they're *that* good. They can be on you like that. Before you even know it. They've even been known to eat leopards. I don't know how they did it. The silver plating over all those ribs."

Curt stands behind Devon to check out the kid's butt and the tapering lines from his broad, angular shoulders. Backs are compelling. The back of a young man's neck is the best of all, but Devon's long hair covers his nape. *Need to see the neck.*

"Let's just top up that drink, and then talk about the position at Emporium. Oh, this is new. This is new. See that mask over there?"

Curt indicates a large, dark wooden mask, a gruesome, leering, fanged face circled by little human skulls. "Picked it up in Katmandu. It's like a god the Buddhists worship. Well, they fear it actually. Sounds like very old testament Buddhism. I forget the name, it scares away evil spirits. Came from a monastery. Smuggled out of Tibet just before the Chinese invaded and ransacked the place. This young guy I met, his grandparents kept it in a trunk. They were storing it for some important lama guy who disappeared. Only took it out and unwrapped it once a year on a certain day. So superstitious, those Tibetans. The old folks died, and this kid needed some cash. He wanted a VCR so he could watch American action movies. Can you imagine what he was willing to give away so he could watch *Batman*? Now – this mask is old. Priceless. He wanted five hundred for it. I beat him down to one seventy-five. One hundred, seventy five, dollars. Priceless. And the best part is – I didn't have to pay any duty. I smuggled it into the country as part of a shipment for the store. No one even realized what this old thing is *worth*."

Devon's glass is empty and his attention wandering. Curt waves the pitcher of screwdrivers in his face.

Potent screwdrivers on an empty stomach render Devon bleary and malleable. *Sure, he could try some modelling. No shit Sherlock. A job does mean doing lots of different things.*

Curt stands in front of the kneeling blindfolded boy. "So you think you're right for the job."

"Yeah."

I'll give him a job. Curt unzips his jeans. *A big job.*

"Are you good with your hands?"

"Sure." The boy smirks, swaying.

"What about chatting up customers, can you smile pretty?"

"Yeah, shure," the boy slurs.

"What else can you do with that mouth of yours?"

Devon says nothing, but licks his lips, his smirk gone. Red pouty lips. *Like a* Details *model, circa whatever year it was. Lots of big-boned baby-faced rough-featured pretty boys with pouty lips, perfect lips to wrap around the Boss Prick.*

Placing his thumb in Devon's mouth, Curt slaps his cock against the side of the boy's pretty young face. Removing his thumb, Curt slides his cock between those luscious lips, enjoying the lad's balking, his trying to get away.

Curt holds the boy's head, not roughly, and slides the sensitive end of his stiff prick in and out of those pouty lips, those perfect, swollen lips that are Curt's to hire, if he so desires, until he gets bored of them and hires a new pretty boy to be his special favourite at the store. He treats his favourite well, while he lasts, stoking the fires of "performance-motivation" with frequent small raises and illusionary promotions – the fire of ambition feeding on the tinder of cheap titles.

STORE QUEEN FOR A DAY is one of the titles bestowed by Saint

James, who plays the role of the reliable martyr at Emporium. With unrestrained dignity, Saint James the Martyr each day grows more tragically bitter, more seriously funny and, yes, more ignored. Occasionally, the odd queer customer loves James dearly and becomes, in turn, the object of *scathingly* dramatic ridicule.

THE TEMP is another recent title James has been using for Curt's special favourite. THE TEMP WHO DOES DICK. AROUND HERE.

When Saint James was shown the new priceless old mask, and offered its story – the story of its acquisition by Curt – he made approving noises. "It *is* a cultural treasure," James affirmed. "And totally effective, too. I don't see a *single* evil spirit lurking anywhere *near* the ugly fucking thing."

"Works like a charm. Ha!" Curt snorted into laughter.

Saint James the Martyr turned then suddenly and laid a cool hand on Curt's meaty overheated arm. "Did you see the fight on the news?"

James' hand flew back to his chest. "I cannot believe we're even *discussing* boxing! Has gay culture come to this? Duh! *Did you see the fight?* But I have to know. Is it just me? In the middle of a boxing match, they're each getting paid a gazillion dollars, and they *stop* it because one of them chomps on the other's ear and then *they really start to fight.* Am I missing something? I mean, isn't *that* what it was all about? Hello! Gladiators! What are you doing! Get *to* it."

A cocksucker and a business expense. Nothing sweeter. In a blurry rush of overlapping details, Curt recalls the succession of hungry, youthful lips employed on his swollen cock. *God, I seem fickle lately. Oh well. Get to it – whatsisname here, on his knees.*

The Relative Bargain

Curt looks down at Devon, at the long, straight black hair spilling over his shoulders, the boy's graceful, shapely limbs and lean track-and-field body. The tip of Devon's boner protrudes from the waistband of the jockstrap. His mouth stretched wide, the angular planes of Devon's face adorn Curt's fat prick like flower petals around a stamen. The mere fact of his cock being in Devon's mouth, although charming and carrying a certain visual appeal, is not enough. The boy is not really working. Not into it at all.

Curt wraps one fist around his cock and grabs the back of the boy's head with his other heavy hand. He bumps the boy's face a few times against his fist on the shaft. *Swelling can only improve those lips,* Curt leers, his teeth showing.

The boy balks, shudders and tries to move away. Curt, worried about his expensive new Tibetan rug, lets him go – the boy was starting to gag and after all, just drank most of a pitcher of sweet screwdrivers. Orange juice, regurgitated, stains.

Never too horny to not *worry about the rug.* Curt chides himself for his lack of feverish spontaneity. *It's only a rug. Only money. The kid was just getting into it.*

Curt likes getting the best deal and the better part of a bargain. *The merchandise in Sri Lanka – there's value for the money. All the boys have to bargain with is youth and beauty and they're too young to know what their scrumptious assets are worth. Plus the competition is fierce. Those poor buggers are desperate. It's a buyer's market.*

In Canada, many boys will not put out, even if you actually give them a fucking job and pay them a couple hundred dollars every week. It's crazy. For two hundred dollars, I could have my own branded slave troupe in Sri Lanka who do that acrobatic aerobic yoga thing all day to keep in shape, and perform for me, motivated as all get-out, all fucking night. That's what I can get for two hundred dollars. Don't have to put up with all the bitchy little poseurs. What does Saint James call it? The AI, the Artificial Intelligence. The Terrible 'Tudes, the attitude, the ingratitude.

Of course, some boys in Canada do put out. And they go far. Curt smirks. *They go all the way. And then I don't even have to give them a job after all.*

Curt herds the boy across the room, guiding him forward with a steadying grip on his blindfold, until Devon is pinned face down into the chesterfield. Anxiously the boy squirms, resisting.

"Relax," Curt says, his weight on the boy's shoulders. "Don't worry. It's okay." Curt rubs Devon's shoulders, massaging the muscles, working along to the boy's neck. His strong hands stroke up from the shoulders into the scalp. Combing through the long hair with his fingers, Curt gently moves it aside, completely exposing the nape. He caresses the bare tapering column with his fingertips.

The back of the neck is where mothers hold kittens to make them relax, so they can be carried to safety. The neck is also where tomcats bite to kill rival offspring, if the warm nest of kittens can be found.

Curt coils his fingers around Devon's neck and tightens his grip. Pulsing with life, the boy's neck was a column of muscle like a snake, a swallowing machine.

With his other hand, Curt strokes down Devon's back and pets his buttocks. Reaching between Devon's legs, Curt tenderly grips the boy's twitching cock, stroking it and gripping the boy's neck and caressing his sensitive body until Devon starts to moan. Curt works his thumb up into the boy's asshole, the rest of his hand splayed over the balls and perineum.

The Relative Bargain

Curt gives Devon's neck a final squeeze then reaches under him and grips his cock. The boy is passive and compliant, as though hypnotized. Curt's meaty hands cover the entire intimate territory from the boy's twitchy shaft to just inside the butt. Sensational territory indeed. A couple of good strokes and squeezes and the prospective young employee arches back, bucks a couple of times, and shoots jet cream all over the Scotchguard, his hole squeezing out a rhythm of quick milking massages on Curt's burrowing thumb.

Curt gets a towel and wipes up the trails of the boy's cum, the creamy globules starting to turn clear, liquify, and run.

Devon sighs, moans, sighs again, deeply, and curls up on the floor.

"I have something for you. A present." Washing his hands, Curt shouts back over his shoulder. "And your present is this – I'm *not* going to fuck you. You'd *like it* too much."

Chuckling, Curt dries his hands on a jacquard tea towel, one of a set he brought back from Sri Lanka, and assesses the prospects of the boy curled up on the floor wearing nothing but a black jockstrap.

Straight boys. Fuck. A waste of good cheap vodka.

Standing at his kitchen island, surrounded by rows of tropical spices he never cooks with, Curt again washes his hands.

WHEN PARROTS BARK

"What good's a parrot who can't even talk?" my father asks again, just to bug me.

Dad brought the parrot home only a couple of days ago, as a surprise. The bird's origins were unclear – Dad said the Amazon. The parrot waddled blinking out of the box and onto my hand, his feet scaly-grey and hot. "I love him," I said loudly, pretending not to notice Mom's face cloud over. "I love him, Dad. I love him." The parrot is gaudy, blue-chested, his head crested with flaming crimson tufts. Brilliant primal colours flicker on his wings and back. When excited the feathers of his crest flare up like exclamation marks, his face flushes, and he barks. He doesn't talk, he barks, and he can growl too, but not convincingly.

"Why is a store open twenty-four hours called a 7-11?" I ask Dad, as we drive past. We need tampons, birdseed, and frozen lasagna. *Three things*, Mom had said. *No need to write it down. Any idiot can remember three simple things.* In the store Dad says, "Look at this bird," handing me a jumbo box of Froot Loops, the toucan crazed with excitement. Dad likes this sweet stuff. Mom refuses to buy it. *Kid's cereal*, she calls it. *Expensive kid's cereal.*

Dad catches me by the shoulder. "We'll just put this in here." He jams a small box of tampons through a slit in the side of the jumbo Froot Loops. "A surprise for your mother."

Fear rises and circles around me, exposing my insides to the world. *He must have made that slit before handing me the box.* I wonder what else he has planned, and check over my shoulders for big round mirrors which see everything. Dad of course has disappeared.

I figure he'll tell Mom I wanted the Froot Loops and Mom will freak out. *I don't know who's worse*, slamming the cupboards and, if she catches your eye, glaring. *That father of yours.* Mom asks why on earth, why go and do something like that? An explanation is never good enough. Dad makes himself scarce until Mom stops asking *Why on earth* and instead says, *Come home.*

I head towards the cash, dragging my feet, feeling slow and heavy and awful, like in that dream where I'm just so stuck and too scared to move.

Again my shoulder is grabbed from behind. This hand is hot and heavy like a thick slab. Turning, I see a name tag pinned to light blue fabric. *Myron, Store Manager.*

Myron is huge. *How does he manage to get around without knocking everything over?*

Myron takes the toucan box. His fat fingers fumble into the slit and retrieve the tampons.

"What's this? A surprise in each box." Large, light blue Myron is so deadpan I don't know if he's joking or not.

Myron guides me to the check-out, where I pay for the birdseed and frozen lasagna. All I can think of is arriving home without tampons. But what can I say? *You know the tampons in the Froot Loops? Mom really needs them. So – can we just go ahead and buy them?*

"Okay," Myron says. "Tell me why you did that."

I feel totally awful – in fact, worse than that. I don't know what to say. I see Dad outside, standing by the car smoking, digging at a rust spot, pretending not to watch me talk to the manager.

Myron hasn't struck me, or yelled. He doesn't even seem pissed off. I feel something pull at me – I really want to tell the truth. (Later, daydreaming doing science homework, I figure this tug of honesty had something to do with gravity because Myron was like so totally gigantic.)

I look at the floor and blurt out, "Dad put them in the box. I didn't know what he was doing, and then, I just didn't know, what to do."

Myron takes a breath, then looks back at me. Like he cares. "That the truth, son?"

"Uh-huh."

Myron sighs again and I look up. He knows everything now. I let out the breath I'm holding.

"Wha'cha gonna do?" I whisper, my voice shaky.

"What do *you* want to do?"

I don't have a clue but suddenly I tell him. "Why don'cha tell Dad you caught me and you're gonna call the cops. That'll scare him." I look at Myron right in his eyes. *What is he thinking?* I turn away and notice my father dragging the last puff of life out of his butt before flicking it aside and elbowing his way back into the store. "Here he comes."

Myron waves Dad over. Sounding very serious, he asks, "This your boy?"

When Parrots Bark

Dad nods, looking at me, all concerned.

"Well," Myron says, "he tried to walk out the store with these" – he waves the tampons in the air and the cashier giggles – "stuck into this box of Froot Loops."

Dad glances at me again. I wait for him to explain to Myron what happened. I smile, watching Myron to see him react as he hears from Dad he was right to trust me.

The slap to my face catches me by surprise. "What are you laughing at," Dad says, fuming. "This is serious, you little shit."

I hold the side of my face with my hand. My head is ringing, spreading outwards, filling my ears, muffling the sound of my own whimpering.

Dad talks to Myron. Can't make out all the words, but stuff like, *Don't worry, take care of this at home. His mother and me'll make him sorry he ever. . . .*

His hand on the back of my neck, Dad steers me out of the store and towards our dirty old car. He opens the passenger door and guides me into the seat like he does with Mom when he's being all mushy. When he's all nicey-nice like that Mom and I roll our eyes at each other before Dad gets in on the driver's side. But now, I just stare down at the bag of birdseed and frozen lasagna between my feet. *We need three things. Three simple things.*

Tampons. Last seen sitting there on the counter next to the box of Froot Loops, the small blue box all calm and serious next to the crazy toucan with the rainbow beak. And the cashier giggling, the braces on her teeth a muted gleaming like dirty chrome.

Dad drives without a word. I want to remind him to stop at another store, but don't say anything.

Almost home, Dad says, "Now straighten up. And stop blubbering. Before your mother sees you."

This is good. This means he won't tell Mom. That it's between us. Like it never happened.

Mom was more upset by the lasagna we bought than the tampons we forgot. *Vegetarian* lasagna did not suit her cravings.

"Typical." She takes a big breath and lets it out, sliding the frozen slab into the oven. "No point asking a man to help out. Surprised you remembered a thing." Standing by the stove she reads the ingredients from the lasagna box. "Hydra, hy*dro*-lized vegetable protein." She snorts. "Didn't I say I was hungry enough to eat a horse and chase the rider?"

I shake out some of the new parrot food. The label showed three birds in a row, each looking chipper and eager. Names run through my head as I watch my parrot pick out the larger seeds. Peanut. Sunflower. *Sunny*. Using his beak and thick round black tongue he shells sunflower seeds faster than I can with both hands. "Sunny," I whisper, trying it out. His neck feathers rustle as he turns his head to watch me with one glistening black eye. I want to touch his soft crown, to stroke the precious little feathers on his forehead, but I'm afraid he'll bite. A parrot can't see too close in front of him.

Dad comes back with really expensive tampons from the corner store and throws them down on the table. The noise startles the parrot, who squawks like a question, rising higher at the end. "A surprise in every box," Dad says.

Bobbing his head, the parrot yaps frantically, like a chihuahua, *wow wow wow wow wow*, and we all laugh. Mom and Dad and I, all

When Parrots Bark

of us laughing. Already the barking parrot is making a difference. He will be a real pet – just like a dog. Maybe I'll give him a dog's name, like Prince. Or Scout. Or Boy.

Sunny Boy. I'll teach him how to talk. I'll explain everything to him and he can repeat it back.

Wow wow wow, Sunny Boy barks. *Wow! Wow! Wow!*

46

THE BOY WHO STOPPED

The knot in his stomach became bigger than he was.

If he ate, the knot grew. Felt like it would burst, except it was too tight.

Instead, he threw up.

So he stopped eating.

He had to be stubborn, but the knot in his stomach is better. Sometimes – it's like it's not even there.

The kids at school are pigs, stuffing their faces every chance they get. Eating for free. Giving it away. It took a big present for him to eat now. A big present – or a big threat.

But the threats have changed, haven't they, Jim? Now I'm too frail, the doctor says. You mustn't touch him. See how things work out, after all?

Now "no TV" is the big threat. He really tries to look like he cares. There's no need to let his mother clue in and find something else to take away. Something that matters.

Like Adam's beret, which he blatantly adored (after he washed it and added a ribbon) and she threw away simply because she couldn't stand seeing it. Couldn't stand seeing the boy prance around all floppy like that.

The boy sleeps and dreams and wakes and feels the core of his body burn bright, hazy but strong. He's never felt so strong as he does now, on the verge of something he's not sure about, and terribly excited.

WHEN FOOD BECOMES THE ENEMY. THE DANGER OF FOOD USED AS REWARD. Concepts from the booklet were blurring in her head.

Food is food, for crying out loud.

Negotiations. Pleading. Tears. She's already been through it all. Bargaining for mouthfuls, haggling over differences.

Counting rituals? His mother threw the booklet down and picked up a cigarette. She didn't need to read more – she lived with this. She sure as hell didn't want the boy to read it, and get any ideas. Next he'll be counting this, counting that. If he starts to count his chewing, she'll never get anything down him.

They might take him away from her. Does he realize that? He seemed oddly triumphant, being taken to the specialist. Like he had won. And couldn't help rub it in, the little bugger.

The boy refused everything she did. His nose turned up now even at poached egg on toast, one of the breakfast-for-dinner dishes which used to work. She had mostly given up cooking. Whatever was easiest, didn't waste much, and made her feel like she was trying. Because she was. She really was.

He always had his reasons, even if they made no sense. The poached egg didn't look right to him, the way it shimmered white and moist and solid. Only minutes before the egg had been translucent slime torn by a lightning bolt of blood, the yolk dull like the early morning sun struggling through a shroud of pollution. Now everything about the egg was solid. The blood was still in there – he just couldn't see it.

"I'll throw up." His prediction was confident, almost cheerful. "If I eat that, I'll throw up."

The blood-streaked yolk fed the embryo. The whole thing was a baby chicken. The boy refused to touch one spoonful of congealed baby chicken blood.

His mother took a breath, inhaling her threats. The book said to separate facts from feelings, but the fact was she was pretty pissed. Maybe he could just eat some toast. Three bites. She felt sick at her urge to shake this stubborn, maddening child, his ears jutting from his thin scalp, blue veins tracing the line of his set jaw. Surrounded by darkness, his large eyes gleamed, even larger now. His eyes glowed with a clear light of such beauty it stole words away. Her whole life was in those eyes. Still, caught by their immense clarity, she could be persuaded not to worry.

Everything had become too much. She used to admire his determination – up to a point, of course, beyond which he drove her insane. But now, he was burning up inside using little more than his own fierce spirit for fuel. This had to stop. It simply had to stop.

"Each meal may seem like a battle," the eating disorder specialist had said, popping a fresh nicotine chicklet into his mouth. "Battles you win or lose. Focus on winning the war."

The boy's mother hated being reminded that the war was her

The Boy Who Stopped

son's life, felt gravely ill herself hearing terms like *kidney failure, organ damage, permanent consequences*. As if she had never thought about permanent consequences. She was already worried half to death.

The specialist practised with several others in an office whose decor was a generic salmon and grey. The prim, chipper receptionist acted just a little too snippy. They weren't used to boys in that office, she commented, glancing at our boy already engrossed in a back issue of *Chatelaine*. Normally, only girls struggle with their appetites. "Mostly girls," the receptionist clarified.

"Mostly girls is still some boys," his mother said. "You're used to *some boys*, aren't you?"

The receptionist smiled smoothly. "Please take a seat." His mother felt deflated. She had puffed herself up and hissed out indignation, only to be told off by a thin, cutting smile, the receptionist as sleek and certain as a weasel.

In the waiting room, the food pyramid poster hung like the weight of dread on his mother's shoulders. Tons and tons of food petering out to nothing. Slaving away for this.

The wait of dread.

The specialist spoke in a monotone. The simple recipe was equal parts manipulation, encouragement, and coercion, but results were frustrating. His head was bulbous, as if his collar had been too tight for too long, and his tobacco-stained fingers fidgeted with a sleek stainless steel pen. Words poured past her, *behaviour mod, denial resistance exploration commitment*. Who in their right mind would even dream of specializing in children's anorexia? Nothing made sense. The best frigging country in the world and the kids would rather starve.

The specialist had been a shock. Their family doctor was concerned. The kid was bruised, but you know how boys are. He just took forever to heal. His weight had been the same, more or less, low normal, for a long time. Very low normal, the doctor emphasized, and at his age, a lack of progress was akin to taking steps back. Diplomatic forays skirted around a conclusive encounter with blame or neglect, but conveyed the flavour of threat. There was the implication that this was her last chance. *Outpatient, family nutrition, trial period.* Her head snapped up at *residential facility* and her doctor had assured her it would *never* come to that.

And so, that's why she took him to the specialist, although sometimes she wishes that they had never gone.

The specialist changed everything.

Children in the waiting room with foreign-born nannies were easy to explain: parents too busy, in orbit, selfish. Those bored, arrogant, standoffish, demanding children had neglect written over them as large as logos.

It was the child with her frazzled mother who upset her. That child was the one who made the boy's mother feel angry and resentful and wish she had never came. Knobby joints too large for thin limbs, skin translucent, sunken eyes in dark fields – the sight of that stick-figure of a child had seized her, and overwhelmed her, and she hadn't been able to look at her own son the same way since.

A phase, is what she had been calling it. A stubborn phase. But her boy had those same eyes. Her baby boy, with his quirky flair and peculiar energy – he was one of *them*, a freakish, skinny raccoon kid asking for dead kidneys or worse if he didn't snap out of it.

The Boy Who Stopped

She was scared, because he was so stubborn. His spark and his stubbornness, bless his heart, now he scared her.

"Have a bath and go to bed," she said with mock firmness. "No TV for you, young man."

When his mother checked on him, he was singing in the tub. Naked except for one of her old bandannas tied around his neck. She looked at the bandanna instead of his corduroy ribs. She caught herself scanning his thin limbs for downy hair, a symptom she had just read about. *What was the word? Laguna? Beluga?* He did have trails of silky hair as white and fine as dandelion fluff. But he always had that. *She* had that. And that bandanna. Can't he ever dress down?

"Why are you wearing . . . that?" (She didn't dare say it looked like a bib.)

"The ascot," he said, all blasé. "That's just Jim Dandy."

"In the bath?"

"That's just *Jim* Dandy!" He repeated, then laughed, sloshing in the waves of his exuberance. Even painfully naked, he was spilling over.

She looked into his eyes to avoid looking at anything else.

Jim inspired him, conspired with him, dared him on. Jim was his mirror, his confidant, his companion. When he saw him in his head, when he felt him inside, he just glowed. Jim glowed. Jim was the only one who truly understood the need for a neck treatment in the bath.

And so their game evolved. The first rule was, never mention the game. The second rule was, if she wanted to watch him eat, there was a price. Every mouthful cost her.

Knowing he was eating in secret was a great consolation for his mother. Patterns evolved around the unspoken rules. She left out food and he secretly disturbed the stash. She was constantly reassured. There was no problem: he was just very strange, very private. An awkward age, not really a child anymore, but still not anything else. And moody. Either jumping up and down in your face or totally listless. He threw people off and made them awkward too.

She baits her traps and checks later for signs of nocturnal life. Raison boxes left out in a pile, packages of biscuits and granola bars opened. To be most tempting, a package should be "in between" – neither fresh and full nor almost gone. *In between* packages can be pilfered, and nothing missed.

She was proud that she never gloated when bait was taken.

Well, hardly ever.

Words the boy would never use: quality time, sanctuary, rituals.

Eating, by himself, unobserved, were all those things. He sang a private grace: *Food for me, no one feeds; me, me, no one sees. Seeds for me, no one feeds.*

Arrowroot biscuits were his favourite. The chubby baby on the box made him feel a kind of secret, delicious guilt.

Arrowroots were decorated with a star-burst pattern around a Greek key design like interlocking boots. He took his time, licking the edge delicately, nibbling moistened crumbs while trying to preserve the points of the stars. The dry, shallow flavour blossomed in his mouth. Once the stars were melted he nibbled all around the boots. The slower he went, the less he tried, the better. Patience was the key. Patience and determination.

Ice cream could have been his favourite, except ice cream had its own rules. Ice cream disappeared from the carton, but never filled the belly. Ice cream could not be replaced or controlled. He promised himself, just one spoonful, but it was never that. Ice cream was never "one."

Ice cream was sneaky. Ice cream made him and his mother both obviously sneaky.

She felt triumphant discovering spoon-hewn craters, the chocolate half-gone from a brick of Neopolitan. She used to be disgusted at the thought of someone eating right out of the carton. Now it reassures her. It's funny how things will flip.

WHEN YOUR CHILD HAS AN EATING DISORDER. When Your Child: there's three words for bad news. It was never, like, *When your child . . . wins a trophy!*

Binge and purge: the words flew in and she suddenly saw the whole story. Now that she knew, it was incredibly obvious. Eating in secret and puking in secret. It was hard now even for her to believe she could not have done the math in such a simple equation.

Everything was coming back at her. Cognitive behaviour therapy – first step, write down everything he ate. As if feeding the world's fussiest brat wasn't enough. Now she had to write down everything he didn't eat, all her crappy meals in a list: Things he wouldn't choke down to save his frigging life.

Separate facts and feelings, *and* put up with hearing, "Please don't take this personally, but your son needs to feel loved."

Told to rock him. Hold him in your arms and rock him in a rocking chair. Christ, like I need to be told how to do this. See, this is all my fault, right. Like I never sat up with him all those nights, him all red in the face and screaming. And later, when he started having those nightmares, the dream demons he called them. Dream demons. Too scared to sleep. Couldn't be left alone. Adam said I babied him, said I'll give him something to cry about if he don't shut up. If I stayed with the boy, Adam would work up a rage in the other room. He could sulk big, and then I'd have the two of them on my hands. The boy and him – it was nasty by then, not like it had been, when things were going better for Adam.

The boy too was nicer, she remembered with a jolt of recognition. He used to be way nicer. He used to be a charmer, before he stopped.

Oh here it is – lanugo. Soft downy growth, sometimes found on the body of a fetus. Her baby does not have laguno. What is it? – la-NOO-go. He doesn't have that. She was flooded with conviction.

This too shall pass. And what's another chore – she already gave up her life. She literally almost died for this kid.

How could this, *this*, be her doing? Who could love him more? No one has loved him like she has and now they say, he needs to feel loved. A flaming dagger twisted into her heart couldn't feel worse than that news. Well, thank you very much, Doctor Nic Fit. He could take his family counselling and shove it up his cognitive blah blah.

When Adam was around it was hard to know who was in the kitchen at night. The boy was better at hiding his tracks, rinsing and drying and putting away the evidence. That itself would be the clue: someone else had done a lick of cleaning. Adam never lifted a finger, just set his dirty bowl next to other dishes, like it was hidden there, camouflaged. It was almost laughable, how stupid men thought women were. How stupid men thought. Would be funny if it wasn't so damn serious.

The boy is suspicious of the idea of rocking. "Why," she says, "because it'll be fun." When he finally climbs on board, he's all elbows and attitude. His whole attitude was sensitive. Resentments jut out, awkward tender bits bristling and easy to bruise.

Too sensitive is basically why Adam had to leave. Adam had been around long enough to be called the stepdad, or the boyfriend, depending on who was asking. Adam's temper, as unpredictable as it could be, had developed a pattern. The pattern was the problem. The boy you see, depending on his mood, could be sullen, or he could be lippy. He could say the cruelest things. The problem was the combination of mouthy on the one hand, and short-fused on the back-hand. Adam found it infuriating how full of himself that boy could be. And, there was that sissy thing, just another phase, but Adam had no time for it.

Sullen and volatile: the household was set to detonate, and Adam didn't want to be around for the repercussions.

A good clean break, is what Adam called his rather abrupt departure.

But for the boy who stopped, the break was not so clean, nor even a break. Life with his mother was much the same in different ways. The boy and his mother still sat in the same chairs at the table.

Across from his cranky, distracted mother, the drugstore fliers collected in front of an empty chair.

If she looked at him at all, he wished she hadn't.

Nobody cared what he did anymore, and with no one to outrage, neither did the boy.

Then Jim Dandy stirred him up and together, they became fashionable. In other words, style was everything.

Jim was opinionated and never satisfied. At the heart of flamboyance is *boy*. And the rest, Jim Dandy advised, is all about refinement. And refinement is up to you. Don't forget – gold can come out of gravel. You can take anything, *anything*, and do something with it. Turn it around. Flaunt it. Use it. *Something*. You take what you're given and work it into something pure and glittering, hard, simple and dazzling, like a diamond.

A diamond was just a rock, the boy knew. Just a chuck of carbon with all the rocky parts peeled away, and what you are left with, is the brilliance. All the extra bits just made things dull. They kept the rock from being a diamond.

The boy no longer talked out loud to himself, except in a whisper. The timbre of his own voice disturbed him. His voice sounded to him like a woman's, distressed and cracking under the pressure.

The boy had super special favourite outfits, although he tried not to. If you cared, you just got hurt. Clothes disappeared overnight, mysteriously; were ruined in the wash; ripped at school; or worst of all – our boy outgrew outfits, inevitably.

The Boy Who Stopped

It was wrong to get attached, because things only let you down. Clothes were treacherous that way.

He loved his brown corduroy trousers, brown like café au lait with a thin precise wale. Suddenly his bony ankles protruded like the dots anchoring exclamation marks. The ignorant pig children displayed absolutely no flair, but did possess keen eyes for detail. *Hey, fruit! Expecting a flood?*

The boy stopped listening to their taunts.

He found some brown and ivory striped canvas and sewed delicately flared additions to the cuffs of his corduroy trousers. The horizontal stripe created a dialogue with the vertical wale, the whole look accented by an innovative neck treatment of the same new fabric.

"Now *this* – is something," he whispered. In his mother's full-length mirror, he was a fall collage of colour and texture. Jim was speechless, then enthusiastic. It was bold. Masculine. Assertive. A red velour long-sleeved sweater with pointed collars. His special brown cords, with new striped cuffs swirling about his feet like action marks around a cartoon character.

Don't even look at the shoes you can't do anything about.

He fussed with the material at his neck, which although a bit stiff, did look jaunty, almost sporty.

Something about this outfit gave him confidence. He felt good, almost new. He felt better outside than he did inside. Maybe, through a process akin to osmosis, that lured him out. He felt so good he forgot himself and told Bruce Lafleur what he should never have mentioned.

He knew better than that, but it was too late to fix.

He was wearing his brand new favourite outfit when he rounded a corner and Bruce Lafleur was right there, leaning against the wall. Our boy stopped cold. Bruce was dangerous. He ran wild. Saggy-ass jeans always torn, sweaters puckered with burrs. Cuts and scrapes were worn like merit badges. Bruce would be bleeding and not even care. During class Bruce picked at scabs, and at recess tried to hand out dark twisty hairs. "Fresh plucked," he called out. "Get yer fresh hot dick weed." Almost a head taller than the other boys, Bruce's body was bursting out of itself, straining the planes, transforming into a very different animal. Our boy couldn't stand Bruce Lafleur and couldn't stop looking at him. Did Bruce Lafleur really have that much hair? Down there?

Anyway, Bruce was right in front of him, leaning against the wall, and he said, "Whaddy ya know?"

Our boy never knew how to answer. "Lots," he whispered, humbly.

"You don't know shit about nothing," Bruce said, but in a nice way, and our boy was touched that Bruce Lafleur was even speaking to him.

"I know stuff," our boy said.

"Yeah, what?" Bruce was smiling.

"Gaydar." The word was said before the boy knew what he was saying.

"Gaydar?"

"Like on Oprah." Bruce's eyes trapped him. The boy whispered, "I know what gaydar is."

Bruce looked stunned and then, filled with knowing he'd been given something.

Our boy was hopeless.

The Boy Who Stopped

He never, ever meant to tell Bruce so much. He had meant to earn respect. He meant to brag about having a special power, like he was a tiny little super hero. He was special. He had gaydar. He was pretty sure of it.

He never thought how it would backfire.

Bruce and Curtis and Peter and Eddie reacted twice.

First they were jealous. *That's stupid. He's not special. How can he have something we don't?*

Then, they realized something. They realized they were that close to being jealous of a sissy. A sissy who made shit up.

After that, it was easy. *He's not special. He's a fag.*

Even fags don't have gaydar, Curtis had heard. *It's just something fags made up cuz fags think they're special.*

And so, without meaning to, he opened his mouth and became a fag.

The boy who stopped eating also stopped talking.

Since he stopped eating and talking, there dwelled a faint, persistent ringing inside his head. Not from his ears, exactly, but between his ears, low from his throat like a growl, and filling the weight of his thoughts. This prevented a lot of other stuff from getting in.

Stuff like, *Skinny sissy faggot fuck, get outa my face.*

Stuff like that, the boy who stopped scarcely heard anymore.

What he heard was a low droning, a warm buzz with no message which drowned out the rest. He clung to the noise with no message, he focussed on it. And walking. Walking wasn't that easy anymore. He had to pay attention to every step.

The pig children regarded his slow progress with horror.

You know, Jim, this is really working out well, the boy thought, as he finally reached the door to the school. *If we're unsteady on our feet, no one knocks us down.*

The Boy Who Stopped

THE BROCHURE

"Shouldn't you buy a car seat, anyway? Just in case?"

"The car seat, the baby's room, the trust fund for college – it could all go in the brochure."

"Have you seen Ivan and Edward's brochure?"

"Didn't they just adopt?"

"Two months ago. A little girl."

"What's her name?"

"Anna."

"This is the prototype but you get the idea."

"Needs a proofreader."

"Tons of grammar mistakes."

"Wouldn't a birth mother worry they'd bring the kid up illiterate?"

"Probably wouldn't notice."

"Anyone ready for a mimosa?"

"Mimosa! Over here! What do you think of this photo of us with the dog?"

"Who's the target audience?"

"Typically – low-income single mothers-to-be."

"Did you mention the house?"

"The house is a selling point."

"Where did you get these bagels?"

"Benny's. It's not our first choice, but we're considering an 'open' adoption. It increases our chances."

"What's an open adoption?"

"Basically – a couple of letters a year, maybe a visit."

"Apparently some birth moms like the idea of gay men as parents. No other woman in the picture to replace them."

"Plus we're younger. Most heterosexual couples try for years to have a baby, then give up and adopt."

"What's it cost?"

"The consultant's retainer is eight thousand for a year. About ten to twelve thousand in total for an adoption within the state, much more outside."

"How many clients does she have?"

"Places fifty to ninety a year."

"Ninety at eight thousand a pop."

"That's just what she places. Retained by more than that. Has a staff of four."

"Not bad."

"She's doing okay."

"Lox?"

"Why don't you just do it on the Web?"

"Because it's, like, illegal, to buy babies."

"Oh my god – you made muffin caps!"

"Yes, made them and burned them. We're trying to pick out more photos of each of us with kids. Shows we're used to being around children, our kid will have playmates, there is an extended family in place."

"Look at you – what a kid magnet!"

"Two summers ago at Ogunquit. My nephews and some of their little friends."

"Did I tell you? Some kid in Zachary's play group toddled up and bit him on the cheek. His mother had to pry him off. She was *mortified*."

"Oh my god. Is he okay?"

"Some lingering tooth marks. He threw up. He's fine."

"At least the bite marks don't match your teeth."

"The funniest thing was – she was just saying how non-aggressive her little boy is, what a little angel."

"This brochure concept is truly inspirational."

"More french toast?"

"No, thanks. I mean, I should just make one up for myself to hand out to guys I'm maybe almost seeing. Instead of glossing over my tedious personal resume each time, I could just say, 'Let's meet for coffee and exchange brochures'."

"Still you might prefer to make up three or four versions, depending on what needs to be emphasized, just like your professional resume."

"But then I'd have to already know something about *them*, to decide which brochure to hand out. I couldn't just hand over all four versions and say, here, see if there's anything you like."

"Make an educated guess, same as applying for a job. You figure out what they're looking for and show them you have it."

"Employers are a little easier to read than guys I'm maybe almost seeing."

The Brochure

"You know Diane? Bruce and Diane? She keeps crowding me, you know, phoning to chat and trying to make plans even though we just saw them. I feel like saying, 'Sorry, we're not accepting new friends right now, but I'll keep your information on file and if an opening comes up we'll get back to you.'"

"Someone *made* chocolate fudge cake? Who has the *time?*"

"Baking is the *only* way to relax."

"The word gay is fine but avoid *homosexual*. In fact the consultant said to steer clear of any mention of s-e-x. It's fine to present ourselves as a warm loving family, yet we should downplay. . . ."

"None of these photos show you touching."

"Never overestimate the sophistication of the birth mother."

"That's just it. She could be a teenager in a small town somewhere. The abstract concept of a couple of men as parents is okay, but a photo of two guys in love could be disturbing."

"We need to select the right photos to finalize the brochure. The consultant says the text is forty percent too long, and suggested a smaller font to create more white space. I thought that would make it too hard to read. She said I had to get over the idea people were ever going to read it."

"She said that?"

"She said that. Yes. She said the pictures were way more important."

"What about these shots from the wedding?"

"Everyone says we look like two best men."

"I'm sure they mean that in the nicest possible way."

"How long will it take?"

"Longer for gay couples. Could be several months. Or more."

"I thought it was easier to adopt if you're gay. I mean, god, look how many men are in my immediate family."

"Are you guys ready?"

"We're excited."

"So – when are you getting the car seat? The photo could go in the brochure – *Your Baby Here*."

Six months after this brunch, the hosts, a gay male professional couple, adopted a baby girl who is by all accounts absolutely adorable. Their brochure was a complete success.

The Brochure

AGAINST NATURE

THE BOY WHO WORE LEOTARDS

His mother thought bright blue tights were a good idea. Maybe she thought they were long johns, never realizing the colour was wrong, and the fabric too even, a fine, soft, clingy cotton. These blue things were not long johns. But even long johns were geeky. They screamed mama's boy. Only babies who didn't know any better wore long johns.

Didn't she know that?

Didn't she know these blue things were leotards, and leotards were for girls?

It was December, okay, but not that cold. "They're what I bought," she declared, "and there's nothing wrong with them. Now get a move on." She cut him off as he drew breath to protest. "And don't make me tell you again."

This was way back years before anyone knew men would discover their bodies and clad them in spandex. The boy who wore leotards was a pioneer at a dangerous time. This was back when straight boys had the gaydar. An early form of the technology, rough and ready, and in the wrong hands.

Back when straight boys had the gaydar, there was a boy who wore blue leotards to school and things did not go well. As soon as his underwear was uncovered, before gym, word spread fast.

Two older boys, notorious troublemakers, were curiously inflamed. They tracked down the boy who wore leotards to exorcise their disdain.

There was something about that boy, a softness or weakness, a refusal to defend himself, that infuriated the older boys. They couldn't have said what it was, the fuel for outrage didn't seem to add up, but something sparked and kindled violence. A flurry of fists and boots and the boy who wore leotards crumpled to the ground.

A trickle from his nosebleed dripped through his fingers, off his face, landing on his new jeans, torn during recess when he was tripped and his knee hit the pavement. The blue leotard hugged his bruised flesh like another layer of skin, stuck on, scuffed and stinging. Oozing a scarlet stain, purple at the rough edges where it seeped into the fabric.

"Faggot," the pair of boys said again, more of a grunt this time than an accusation, before going off together, kicking the ground and punching the sky.

"They walked in." The boy explained to his mother how the mason jar seething with caterpillars arrived in his bedroom. "I opened the door and they just walked right in."

"One of my good jars," she said, and then looked at him for a long moment. "No bugs in the house." She pronounced this like she really meant it.

No bugs in the house became a new rule.

The boy who loved bugs was surprised to discover that no bugs also meant no snakes.

When she came to say goodnight, his mother spotted the mound under the sheet next to him by the pillow.

"That better not be more bugs," she warned.

"It's not."

"Let me see that."

The boy's mother stopped screaming, becoming almost non-hysterical, once the boy ran outside with the mayonnaise jar and returned empty-handed.

"Did you kill it?" She glared at her son. "I told you no bugs in the house."

The boy was totally surprised. He thought he was being good. A snake would eat bugs. It was no different than having a cat for the mice. He hadn't planned to, but down by the ditch he'd rounded a stand of weeping alders and spied the snake sunning on a rock. The snake tried to melt away but in a quick curious move, the boy snatched it up, grabbing it just behind the head. He'd seen snakes before, of course, but never caught one. Carrying it home, the snake's body twined around his wrist, warming. Stripes mottled with red ran down its length, hinting at a brighter red at the snake's core, as red as the thin tongue flickering in the air, forked, pointed, incredibly neat. Up close, the snake's face looked put together from finely crafted pieces, yet quick with life. Snakes were supposed to hiss, but this one was completely silent. The boy, too, tried to be still, to avoid being picked on for the way he said 's' words, dangerous words like lisp or sissy – like he had too much tongue.

The red fork flicked out, precise and immaculate, the dark pointed tips seeking the very warmth of the air to bring inside to taste.

"No one will hear you," he had promised the snake.

He loved that snake with a passion as absolute as his sense of justice and as naïve as having faith in logic. "But a snake is not a bug!"

"Don't be smart with me." His mother still looked poised for flight. "You know what I meant. And you turn around and bring one of those things right into the house. Are you doing this just to torture me?"

"Snakes don't hurt nothin'."

Something inside his mother snapped. Patience maybe. "Oh, snakes hurt," she yelled. "Snakes hurt a lot."

She started pacing, and suddenly the room seemed too small to hold her.

"Oh, you're getting it now. You are really gonna get it now."

When "it" meant a beating, there was a choice.

The strap was leather and could leave welts. One strap about eight inches long lived in the drawer in the kitchen with the shingle. The boy's father had his own strap, the belt he wore around his waist, keeping it handy in case he needed to lash out. But Dad wasn't home, although Mom certainly expected him to be, quite some time ago. For once the boy hoped to hear the words, "Just wait till your father gets here." That could mean anything. And anything was better than Mom like this, circling and building like a storm.

His mother chose the shingle, which was more her style, lightweight and stinging. The smooth wooden shingle left no mark other than reddening the skin when smacked on bare flesh. A reddening like being on fire.

Strapping at least was measured out by numbers – up to five. Ten was still a threat. The flight of the shingle knew no number. That is what short-circuited the boy, what broke his determination not to care. When he realized that he could not know, could not predict the end of punishment – that is when he started to act like a baby.

His mother didn't have the heart to beat a bawling child for long. The boy knew that, but refused to cry just to avoid a licking. That wasn't proper. It wasn't proper either how his Dad got carried away and went all over the place, striking not just his buttocks, but down his legs and up his back.

At least his mother managed in her frenzy to aim for his butt.

Dad could not be trusted to do that.

The boy who loved bugs was embarrassed, having his pyjama bottoms peeled down and his backside flailed with a worn shingle. Flushed with outrage, he cradled his face in his arms.

The pain did not just erupt into a blazing fire-blossom and then blur into a merciful numbness, no, the flat smack of the shingle laid down the base for a fierce stinging which grew and grew and promised to never fade. Like a bee sting, only a hundred times worse. No, like hundreds of wasps, because they could each sting over and over again.

Against Nature

The boy who loved bugs knew about wasps. He knew about bugs and frogs and toads and snakes. He knew enough to realize nature was trouble.

Singing in the bath when he was no more than three or four, inspired by the easy lifestyle of Bert and Ernie and belting out *Rubber Ducky You're the One* like a show tune from the heart of his soul, the boy's perky exuberance became part of oral tradition.

Except, his family never described the boy who sang when wet quite like that.

They never used words like "perky" or "exuberant" or "show tunes." They never mentioned any oral tradition.

They just said, "He had a way about him, you shoulda seen him sing."

Whenever he overheard them talk, he felt smaller. His need to sing when wet wasn't really something they had words for anyway, but still they talked, cautiously, which made it seem just plain weird, rather than what it was – a kind of natural overflowing. That explained, in a queer way, why singing when wet was shy, reluctant to pass outdoors, out into an early morning salute to the dew, or out into the snow which drifted down and wrapped the world in its peculiar silence. Even running through the sprinklers during a gloriously sombre, big-horizon sunset, the boy did not sing.

Singing when wet changed once the spring floods of puberty washed up over adolescent embankments. He sang outside playing

Frisbee with Max in the rain at the end of a heat wave. They had crouched near a stand of alders in a dry slough to smoke a furtive joint as slender and lumpy as they were. Licking their fingers, they dabbed out fire spreading unevenly. Handed the spit-kissed offering back and forth, a talking stick in a ritual of their own invention. Beads flew from the jut of Max's brow when he jerked away to cough. A thunderstorm threatened in the distance, promising dramatic relief. Wearing only shorts, they ran around, arms and legs flying, the Frisbee flung – and caught – between the legs. Tentative droplets from the heavens mingled with their sweat. Then the cold rain broke and plummeted to the ground. The rolling, raucous throat-clearing of the gods spat thunderbolts, slicing the sky into jagged pieces. "Are we not men, we are Devo," they chanted like robots in the rain. And screamed as the thunder exploded almost with the lightning, the sharp rolling edges cracking loud enough to rend the earth.

The boys collapsed laughing into the mud to wait out the storm, shivering with excitement and the goose-bumped luxury of feeling chilled. No harm can reach euphoria.

The boy who sang when wet sat up. "We gotta clean up," he said. "Let's shower together. To save time."

Max froze, face sharp and tighter. "That would be too weird."

Something shifted. Something never talked about.

Singing when wet became a solitary practice swimming lap after lap with a swim club. Refined through mindless repetition into a bubbly scat, each liquid string flowed into the next breath. Goggles like portholes capped the eyes of the boy who sang when wet and his coach's words mutated into nonsense syllables ballooning past waterlogged ears, "reach out, stretch the stroke, and Christ almighty, guys, don't forget to follow through."

The boy felt immersed in fluids, overwhelmed, they boiled up out of him in the night, leaving dried traces on the wispy hair trailing down his lower belly, like his navel had become the third eye to accumulate crusty bits in the night. Whiffs of the pool clung to him like sheep dip, crisp with a tangy edge, but on the trail of his own scent he was enraptured, secretly fascinated by the persistent pong of armpit, underwear musty with seaweed and sewers, and alone under the covers, rich rank effusive farts.

During preliminary heats at a swim meet in the city at the Sports Plex, he once again failed to qualify. He went to the showers to be alone, the cold tiles an echo chamber amplifying his faint humming. The boy realized this would be his last swim meet. *All those laps and where did it get me?* His asthma was acting up and pool chemicals made it worse. The doctor made a joke of it. "Chlorine was mustard gas, a weapon in the First World War. Now it disinfects and purifies. And fluoride? What's that? Nerve gas to the Nazis. Now it's in our drinking water too."

The mustard gas sat heavy in his chest, a fluid and phlegmy yellow-green. Churning up, choking him back, like all those times he held his breath – a little death. *Our chemical friends guard against contamination.* He dared not let a hint escape of the electric sensation sliding past nearly naked swim-mates, their flesh sleek and slick and cool. But he had been around long enough to know. Some guys were swimmers, and he was not. Swimmers were a different breed. Self-consciously vain, yet totally unaware of being stuck reenacting a timeless, quintessential pursuit: dozens in a puddle swimming like mad, racing to win.

RANDOM ACTS OF HATRED

They're all just trying to fertilize some fantasy. The same little race over and over, and too stupid to see it. Can't see past the end of the lane.

A freestyler from another team, laces dangling loose from his tiny red swimsuit, stepped up to a shower. The freestyler's head was shaved, and he grinned squinting into the spray, one eye gleaming. Looking fresh and naked, a brand new adult, the freestyler started to hum, then let loose with a song, *Failing to Qualify*, a lament about shaving his whole body for nothing. "All that hair, *down* the drain." The freestyler touched his razored chest. "Lots more where, *that* came from."

The boys gazed into each other's eyes for two thudding heart-beats, and then laughed together like fools under the hot needling torrents, and maybe cried a bit – who could tell, in the showers at the Sports Plex. Water poured over the boy who sang when wet, and the words to his coach-song, *reach out, follow through*, stuck tight in his chest. The freestyler was right there, his back a cascade of rippling waterfalls, startlingly compelling, but as in a dream, just beyond reach. *Stretch*. The boy felt his heart hurting, an ache yawning like the distance which separated them. He felt trapped and longed to break free, to – whatever, *change. To not be like this.* He put his head under the water, the spray drilling his scalp and practised humming a new tune. But when he gathered himself together and looked up, the freestyler was gone.

And that was that.

Five improvised minutes they spent together so long ago yet remembered clearly, still, wondering if something should have been different.

Now the boy who sang when wet sings doing dishes, if there's enough of them, and they need to get done.

Against Nature

The boy does his age in minutes on the treadmill. Usually he does twenty-three, or thirty-one. He's tried being fifty-three, but it is tiring.

He'd read about *namba* in the newspaper and thought he'd give it a try. *Namba* used to be the official *samurai* way to walk, until one hundred and fifty years ago when American warships slid into Tokyo Harbour and entered the Japanese *gestalt*. The official *samurai* way to walk was like marching – anyone could do it, if they had to. Left leg and arm forward, both at the same time. It was hard to start, to get the right limbs to move together. The first several strides were self-consciously awkward, but then, like a switch was thrown, he fell into the swing of it, and was able to walk without really questioning what to do next.

Goosestepping, he was, right there on the treadmill, and no one batted an eye. He struggled with his breath, his thoughts jagged. *What if, gays in the military, and no one, cared? What if, people got married, and no one noticed, except friends, and family?* Already he felt politicized. There must be more to this *samurai namba* business than stepping like a goose.

Back when far-flung wings of the family used to gather for the odd holiday, the rule was: *Never Mention Japan.* Yet holidays, with booze flowing and dinner late, turned out to be just the time to bring up the Imperial Japanese Army, and lovingly detail a range of excesses relative to other unfortunate events. What *they* did in China, compared to *us* in Vietnam. Or Cambodia?

Which unnatural disaster was worse? One Thanksgiving his uncle arrived driving a Toyota, "My baby," he called the car. "My

78

brand new baby." At Christmas, his father stabbed the dining room table three times with a carving knife – Mom looked righteously wronged, the succeeding layers of her expression foreshadowing the patch in the tablecloth to be covered by a strategic dish and never mentioned.

The boy who does his age in minutes was supposed to be going through stages of his life, year by year, to see more clearly what has happened. "It's not my parents' fault," he'd told his therapist. "I feel sorry for them. It's not like they'll still have grandchildren. It's harder when the only child is gay."

His therapist had become predictable: "Why are you making excuses for them? This is about you."

The boy on the treadmill wonders about the stages in his therapist's life, ending up as *he* has, male-pattern baldness but no other apparent testosterone, a meek and ordinary façade of self-acceptance, and so relentlessly *earnest* he made the boy anxious for a bit of cynicism or sarcasm – something slick and hard. Superficial, yes, but comfortable.

You, the boy reminded himself. *You*.

Twenty-three was not long enough. His grandfather at twenty-three had already been captured as a POW, interned in Hong Kong, and endured whatever was handed out.

Atomic weapons were tested on the cities of Hiroshima and Nagasaki, and the boy's grandfather, liberated, returned to Canada old beyond his years, haunted by a gaunt, vacant expression which lingered even after he fleshed back out. Granddad kept his suffering inside, but could turn mean in a flash, so folks circled warily, but still, they circled. He drank to keep things inside and he drank to keep people away. He brought the prison camp home with him and lived

Against Nature

in it, and his family – those people closest to him for the rest of his life – they didn't belong there, not where he was; so there was this distance around him. This distance was like a limbo, a gap in the decision between living and dying. This is maybe why Dad turned out like he did – couldn't wait to leave, to get the hell out of there, and when the waves of drama, despair, and restitution finally played themselves out and his circles drew smaller, Dad came back for good, but still resented staying put in the middle of nowhere with a harping wife and a boy who, well, *no son of mine was going to turn out like that. So help me god.*

Young ears hear more than they understand.

The war-scarred man fathered several sons, one right after he returned, and more years later. Dad was the eldest, and referred to his brothers as "the boys."

"You think I'm hard on you – Christ, you don't know the half of it." This is when Dad seemed proud of his father. "When he clobbered you one, you knew it. The boys never had to do a thing. I was the one that stood up to him, and after that, he let us get away with murder. He never bothered a soul after that."

The boy had told the story, many times, of his father coming home late, wound up from drinking and needing to talk. *He wouldn't care that it was me; he'd wake me up, and I'd put on a jacket over my pyjamas and sit in the kitchen and listen to him ramble – not listening really, just sitting there, trying not to do anything wrong, my stomach clenched like a fist. Trying not to attract attention. Trying not to hope. Trying not to disappoint. Trying to be still.*

When Dad's younger brothers – the boys – were old enough, Dad told them what was what. "There was like a shell the old man lived in – and it'd be a shock if he ever came out of it. So we shouldn't bother him. That way, you see, the boys wouldn't go and have any expectations. But they never had a single clue to share between them. They never knew him, I was the only one."

Late at night in the kitchen, Dad dwelled on his brothers, how shallow they were, and gullible, taken in like fools by their father, even going so far as to embrace his flaws, somehow, as icons of character.

"They couldn't figure out nothing," Dad claimed. "He had one quick son, and a slew of slow ones. Christ, he was almost gone by the time they came along. Just someone they could point to and say, yeah, that's the old man, the prisoner of war. Some falling-down old drunk who had suffered for something that meant something a long time ago, and that was enough for them. As dumb as fenceposts. They never knew him like I did, when he would as soon haul off and wallop ya one as look at ya. Lay me out sideways, he would. Before he stopped caring. What anybody did."

Entrails of snot glistened on his upper lip and he reeked of morning after, beer spilt in ashtrays, his breath like hot death. Embalmed, and off-gassing.

"I told the boys," Dad said, "I told them if he was drinking to stay away from him. And if he wasn't drinking – well, we'd cross that River Kwai when we come to it."

Dad harboured a bitter pearl, and the boy wonders, what piece of grit had worked under his skin and managed to become the special irritant?

"They *should have* used him for bayonet practice." That's what Dad said about his father. "The Japs should've *tried* leaving him out in the cold. Too mean to die, he was. He would have showed them." And Dad would laugh then, laugh in spite of himself, laugh

Against Nature

like it was the first time he had said *too mean to die* late at night in the kitchen, his eyes blurring, then rub his face with both hands, his chuckle disintegrating.

He suddenly snarled, "What are you still doing up?" And the boy scurried back to bed, shivering in his jacket, and mulled over the words churning through his head.

Churning fluid and hazy like car exhaust in the cold morning air, as the boy fumbled into his clothes, late for school and sleep-stupid, the words evaporating upon contact. *One quick son. Bayonet practice. Something that meant something.*

While on the treadmill, the boy has eyes only for beauty. That was his compensation: time spent at the gym need never be ugly hour. A delicate-featured buff boy, very *Exercise For Men Only*, does lunges wearing a skin-tight scarlet outfit, like a collegiate wrestler. Very *Dig Me*. A duo spotting each other at the squat rack are perfect for porn. Sleeveless fleece, Body Body, Caterpillar boots. Hairless, and ripe for metamorphosis.

Bookmarks each sight, then scans to make sure he isn't missing something better.

The bulk of the sad parade his gaze glances off, so lightly disdainful it never usually touches.

A large red-faced man flails back and forth on the rowing machine, his balloon head nodding to follow a straining muscular lout doing pull-ups on the Gravitron. The rowing man reminds the boy of his uncle, the Toyota uncle – the same burly girth through the entire torso, legs thin and ridiculous, a combustible complexion. His uncle had been with the Americans in Occupied Japan. The story was he'd fallen in love while over there. Something had touched him, that's for sure, because when he came back, he had his own ideas. He strongly felt the people, the Japanese people, had been punished enough, even before the bombs, and the famine. His uncle would trump any escalating table-talk with "the babies" – born after the war and of consuming interest to the U.S. authorities. "You wouldn't want to know about them." The uncle wiped grease from his face with a meaty paw. "Two heads. Born without skin. Freaks, that's what they were. It was like hell was leaking."

Too gruesome to mention, those babies were – except on holidays, with a dismembered turkey carcass nearly, its thin rack of ribs cradling a moment of stillness.

The boy who does his age in minutes does nothing but *namba* on the treadmill for three solid weeks of workouts. Obsessive tendencies, his therapist noted. "The doubting disease, that's what the French call obsession. Always needing to check, to make sure, to improve."

Control freak, his ex-boyfriend had called him – one of the last things he'd said.

A perfectionist, he was known as, at corporate headquarters.

So. Just over fifty years since America occupied Japan, kept the Emperor and installed democracy. There is this boy in North America, a young man really who practices *namba* on the treadmill, marching like no one else. He does his age in minutes wearing tight blue Lycra, the colour deep and rich, with a satiny luster. Waiting in his locker with his suit is a new tie clip, an iridescent-armoured, ento-mology collectible.

"If it weren't for my obsessions," he confided to his therapist, "I'm afraid I wouldn't have any personality at all."

His tie clip, a dark metallic-green stag beetle with subtle rain-bow overtones, rests in the locker while the boy does his age in minutes on the treadmill.

"Do you really remember that boy?" his therapist pressed him. "Or are you just telling me stories *about* him?"

The electronic fusion of jungle house pulses on his headphones. He was going for thirty-seven, but maybe he'll do thirty-one instead. It had to be a prime number. Prime numbers are special, and he knew there were fewer of those as you age. Thirty-one, plus a short warm down. Right left, no, right *right*, struggling with the split be-tween this side and that, struggling with the coordination required just to keep going.

THE COMPASSION CLUB

Victor stopped to chat with beggars in Acapulco. And gave them money, especially to women in shawls holding limp, docile children with their heart-breaking eyes.

Over lunch at an oceanside cantina, David was annoyed enough to ask, "Why do you bother with those – those black velvet people?"

Victor picked at his grilled red snapper. "They give me something too," he stated. "Like I've bought something. Really – they're compassion vendors."

David spewed out beer, spraying the *ceviche* he'd insisted on ordering and then set aside as suspect. (He thought it smelled bad, but who could tell? The whole place smelled bad.) David wiped his face with a napkin. "Compassion vendors my ass. They treat you like a bank machine. Push your buttons and get some cash."

"No, I mean –" Victor paused. "I mean, they may be beggars but they provide the luxury. They allow me to be generous. They make me feel rich. They allow me to feel compassionate by giving away such a little bit."

David ordered another Dos Equis. "I'm sure you mean well, but in fact, you were richer before you wasted your hard-earned money on some slutty little señorita."

David smiled broadly to show he was joking and truly did understand. He helped himself to a couple of Victor's hand-cut fries, then leaned back. "We are here," he said, spreading his arms wide. "We are really here."

David preferred to spend his pesos parasailing. Rigged into a rectangular parachute like a kite towed by a powerboat, he soared one hundred and fifty feet above Acapulco Bay, the terrain opening up beneath him, ripening into a panorama.

"I have too much respect for gravity," Victor said. "If they run out of gas, you'll drop like a stone."

"I'll just drift down, a little splash in the ocean."

"A little splash all over a rock."

"You worry too much." David pooh-poohed whenever Victor fretted.

David was diligent in his research to select the best crew. The three he chose were young and handsome and quick to smile. Their friendliness made the difference. There were better bargains on the beach, but David sought the complete package. The athletically trim young man who strapped him into the harness had vivid green eyes, black curly hair, and white white teeth. The other two, the boat crew, had to be lovers: David felt strongly that he was not just imagining things. The green-eyed young man touched his hips and thighs and back somewhat more than necessary while adjusting the parachute straps and the life jacket. ("A great strapping lad," David described parachute boy later at home, skewering the Mexican vacation into tasty, tantalizing morsels. "Parasailors, Acapulco – always an explosive combo!")

"To go dees way," parachute boy said as he touched one side of David's pelvis, "lean from the hip." Parachute boy pushed out his own hip with the same emphasis he used to pronounce *heep*. "Like dees." He put both hands on his hips. "Like dees, or dees."

"You go both ways?" David was almost giddy at his audacity.

"Depends . . . which way . . . you wanna go." They both laughed, the balance of innocence restored.

The boat cruised out slowly while the green-eyed young man and his many sudden assistants spread out the chute and readied for lift-off. As the tow line grew taut and the gentle onshore breeze filled the parachute with a billowing snap, David lifted into the air, suddenly buoyant. The crowded beach shrank away beneath him. High above the bay, he flew out *La Bocana*, the Big Mouth, as far as *Punta Bruja*, Witches' Point. The boat powered into a wide turn and David surveyed the hotels lining the beach and development creeping like a skin disease up the mountains. From dramatic perches on ocean-side cliffs, gleaming aqua-blue swimming pools anchored manicured terraces. The whole grand sweep of ocean and islands, the pools of wealth and poverty, were all arrayed beneath David. At this height, the wind in his face was refreshing, a cleaner tang hinting at open water, instead of laden with overripe rot, sweet sewage, and exhaust.

Banking back through the harbour, the powerboat slowed to a final swoop parallel to the beach. David settled down into the warm shallow water, grabbed and steadied by the outstretched arms of the green-eyed youth.

Victor and David had rented a spot on the beach, their home away from the hotel. It was only a little more money, so why not? Beach chairs, table service, an umbrella that looked like a giant sand mushroom, its thick wooden stem surmounted by a circular thatched cap. They swiftly redecorated by throwing bold tropical fabrics over the chairs and for ambience always referred to their encampment (as listed in the surcharge brochure) as the "palapa." (David said palapa was Spanish for "biodegradable furniture." "Such an economical language," Victor had replied.)

David flopped down next to Victor at the palapa. "How was it?" Victor asked politely, looking up from Henry James and offering the bottled water.

"Fun. While it lasted. But over too soon."

"Like sex."

David grunted. "I can always go again."

"Yes." Victor returned to *The Turn of the Screw*. "Just like sex."

"My, isn't this a big beach," David drawled pointedly. "I'm sure there must be compassion available. Somewhere." He slathered sunscreen on his shoulders and launched himself up for a stroll along the water's edge. "Gonna find me a compassion vendor."

In *The Turn of the Screw*, characters disfigured by emotions are described as "ugly and queer." Victor wondered if queerness today was still a type of emotional disfigurement. *And gay too, was it essentially emotional?* Victor's attention had perked up at the mention of the children's guardian, their gallant, splendid uncle, a bachelor in "the prime of life," "handsome and bold and pleasant, off-hand and gay and kind."

As are many of our kind, Victor thought, watching David schmooze with beach vendors.

David was lean, still, Victor noted, with a familiar twinge of envy. *And tanned too, of course. Always tans just like that, looking more Mediterranean by the minute.* Victor sighed and adjusted the wide brimmed straw hat he wore even in the shade of the palapa. He was itchy, blistered, and bound to peel. It surprised Victor mid-winter how quickly the touch of the sun turned hostile, searing his grub-pale flab into a fierce swollen carapace the colour of boiled lobster. The first day on the beach, awakening from a short intense nap, the sight of Victor's burnt bulk had caused David to shriek. Victor looked enormous, like a beached whale, only *so red*. "But don't you worry," David said, grasping Victor's arm, leaving an angry white impression. "Tomorrow on the beach, we'll find even fatter people and hang out next to them. No one will notice a thing. I promise. Now, let's go lather you up with aloe."

"Ola! Ola!" As David made his way down the beach, the handsome trio of parasailors waved him over. They sprawled around the powerboat gently rocking in the shallows and with chitchat came laughter and some knowing nudges. The green-eyed young man, in a moment of great humour, squeezed David's thigh. Swept along by the camaraderie, knowing he was being milked but feeling too silly to care, David had to admit that, yes, another glorious spin around Acapulco Bay would be *perfecto, splendifico*, whatever.

A panorama can be as compelling as heartbreak. The experience lures and beckons, then the moment peaks, and slides past, and even if the descent is not a crash, the higher you soar the further to fall, back into the grit and struggle, into the stench and desperation, and into the strong musky arms of the green-eyed young man – who is so gorgeous that David stumbles in the wet sand.

Beauty may be fleeting, but it still manages to create a stir.

Strangers wondered years ago if David and Victor were brothers, when their promise was fresh and flush with the easy giggles of love's early bloom.

Now their bonding cycles are complete and they've been friends forever. No one asks if they are related.

Anyone with a hint of worldliness who gives it a moment's thought assumes they are sisters.

On the flight back to their frozen, squalid provincial capital, many miles north of Acapulco and dreary beyond description, David orders a double G & T.

"Two Gees, one Tee," he says brightly to the ruggedly-handsome-yet-sensitive steward, hoping for a mirroring acknowledgment. The steward is perfectly courteous but unwilling to flirt.

David fidgets with his drink and downs a series of furious sips. "They're not really making them straight these days, are they?" He twirls his eyes up and back to indicate the male flight attendant who had maintained a cool professional distance.

Victor's new mantra is a plea for serenity: *May my will be at one with God's will.* He often finds himself teetering on the thin edge between tolerance and exasperation. The ties that bind are a test of patience. He smiles at David. *A day at a time* may sound simple and straightforward, but there are long patches covering bleak, featureless days where nothing is manageable except his breath. Breathe in.

RANDOM ACTS OF HATRED

Breathe out. That was all he could do. How simple is that?

Leaning back against the headrest, David turns and blurts, "Were you that bored, Victor?"

Victor suspects a trap, and takes a breath before asking, "What do you mean?"

"What do you mean what do I mean?" David feigns indignation.

"Well–" Victor bites the bullet. "Do you mean was I bored, or was I boring?"

David hesitates about his choice of words, then *fuck it*, takes the bull by the horns. "You used to have fun, Vic. Fuck. You used to let your hair down."

"Oh, I had fun, David. I somehow managed not to be bored in paradise, David. And *I* didn't spend all my money. Did you have fun, David?"

"Jesus, *Victor*. You can be such a prick, *Victor*."

Conversation fell into a lull. Neither is pleased the trip is over. Mexico was a vacation from winter as much as anything else, a trip to a warm affordable world (with some scenes of poverty too overwhelming to do anything about, personally, which was both humbling and liberating). Seduced by the gentle surf, the heat, the casual comfort of shorts, sandals, and T-shirts, the naturalness of *salsa piquante* even with breakfast: David and Victor had slipped into believing that summer would last forever. *Life is a beetch*, David said late last night, faced with the need to pack. His sneering made leaving seem like their choice. Everything about Mexico was crap. And the smell. That fucking smell *was* Mexico. He wouldn't miss *that*.

David orders another serious drink, treating the steward like scum. Settling in with headphones to watch the movie, David joins

The Compassion Club

the scattered community, on this plane, who react together at intervals: laughing, gasping, laughing again with relief.

Victor sips coffee and struggles with Henry James, determined to finish the damn thing and get it over with. The cover promised a mystifying psychological puzzle: *Are the children innocent? Or, do evil ghosts have power over them?* It was also described as short, but it dragged and endured. The puzzle to Victor was why this was considered a masterpiece.

Just before they land, the plane shaking and skittish, struggling to slow down enough to touch the earth, David places his hand on Victor's leg, much like the green-eyed young man had squeezed his thigh. "Well, we're here," David says.

"Yes we are." Victor places his hand over David's.

Landings make them both anxious.

Back at home, real life swept them up in a mad struggling rush of routines in the face of nasty weather. Mexico faded faster than artificial tan lines. David phones, bored and antsy. "Let's go out Friday. We haven't been to Buffoons in so long. C'mon, Victor. It'll be a slice."

"Okay," Victor says, surprising them both.

On Friday David arrives at Victor's bubbling with excitement.

"Perhaps I am easily exhilarated. But this is a true thrill. A new drug dealer! So convenient!"

"It's not that you're easily exhilarated," Victor says. "Just so often."

"You're looking good," David says. "Have you lost weight?"

"Why – do I look less fat?"

"Oh, give it a rest." He offers Victor the skunky joint. "Sure you don't want any?"

"Not if we're going out. Paranoia I prefer in small private doses." Victor sighs. "Where did you get this stuff anyway?"

"You will not believe this. I heard about this guy, you know, just as a good source. I went and it was like a compassion club. Not *the* Compassion Club, it was like a business too but also like, a compassion club. The guy asked me, he said, *I understand this is for medicinal purposes?* And I thought, *Better say yes.* So I got the special price. Who cares if he thinks I'm positive? I couldn't be more positive. It's organic and cheap!"

Victor is speechless at the coincidence. Is this synchronicity – a message from the universe? Just last week Victor's doctor mentioned, almost as an aside, that some people find marijuana helps with the nausea and can bring back an appetite.

"The munchies," Victor said, absently, almost reverently.

"Yes." His doctor smirked. "Remember the munchies?"

Victor felt a rush of guilt, for having enjoyed eating.

"I could write a note," the doctor offered. "You could try the Compassion Club."

Victor was tempted but just said no. On his way home he realized he didn't even know how to find the Compassion Club.

Now David has stumbled across one, or is he telling the truth?

David is desperately trendy, and known to lie. And known to lie about lying, yet is easily offended if not believed. To his credit, he's also been documented right in the middle of outrageously true events, so when it comes right down to it, it's hard to tell.

"Organic and cheap, eh?"

Finishing the joint, David speaks without exhaling. "If I ever need compassion, I'll just go get some. It's so civilized. If only the baths were that easy."

The Compassion Club

"Maybe at the baths you're approaching the wrong people. If there's already a line up, stud-boy doesn't need your, ah, *compassion*. Try one of the lonely old guys."

"Ew." David wrinkles his nose and coughs out a pungent cloud.

They head out to "Buns & Puns" at Buffoons. The club used to be a Greek family restaurant, with stucco arches, red checkered curtains, hanging baskets of plastic plants, and a stage off to one side for a three-piece *bouzouki* band. Now the Buffoons concept is "male entertainment." A stand-up comic named Loo ("as in Looky Loo") introduces go-go dancers and tosses off jokes, his deadpan delivery a sharp contrast to the full-on nudity.

"All that's left of the Souvlaki Palace is the stucco and the stage," (the comedian pauses) "and hot sticks of meat. Instead of plastic plants we have baskets hung with plastic implants. But the crowd hasn't changed – still active Greeks."

No one laughs, except for a few tentative chuckles from new people. Loo has ran his Greek material into the ground. With any encouragement, he'll trot out hoary old jokes: *In ancient Greece, how did they separate the men from the boys? – With a crow bar.*

"So," Loo continues with the low key enthusiasm of someone who knows he deserves a cult following, "What did one gay sperm say to the other gay sperm?"

David and Victor flash at each other. "Beat you," Victor says. "Get outta my face?" David says.

"What did one gay sperm say to another gay sperm?" Lou makes swimming gestures in front of his wrinkled-up face. "How can you find an egg in all this shit?"

RANDOM ACTS OF HATRED

The audience groans.

"Okay, okay, keep your pants on. I'm just filling in between costume changes at a strip club. You won't be seeing much of *me*."

Looky Loo is a sad character whose act is based on looking forlorn and neglected. David hates Looky Lou. David could walk into a room half full of older, faded men and report (with obvious dismay and not a trace of irony), *No one is here*.

"You know what my problem is?" Looky Loo says. "My problem is I *forget* to masturbate. I phoned a buddy and said, what did'cha get up to on the weekend? He said, oh not much, just stayed home and masturbated. I thought, jeez, stayed home *and* masturbated – why didn't I think of that?"

The crowd laughs for the first time. Loo almost smiles. "My buddy said, even his cum towel has a stiffy. His cum towel *stands* in the corner until he needs it. I thought, *cum towel*? What's that?"

"My, isn't he droll," Victor says.

"Did you say droll or troll?" David laughs louder than he did at Loo's jokes, then is suddenly exasperated. "*Loo* must be short for *lewd*." David is impatient for his current all-time favourite. For many go-go dancers, the stage showcases the product line, but David was just looking, not shopping. David preferred the thrill of the hunt. There is no thrill when the prey stalks you with a price list. Revved up by the pretty boys at the bars, David would head off to the baths to try his luck bagging a big-game trophy in the wild.

A performer at Buffoons is not always a hustler marketing his assets, but *duh*, he might be underemployed. Here at Buffoons, art compels dancers to end up buck-naked and their climax can be spectacular, especially if new and enthusiastic and become a little carried away. (That's how one local legend made his first big splash, spraying a cascade of opalescent liquid jewels across the footlights, casting his pearls before swine.)

"And here *he* is," Looky Loo announces. "A man among men – he stood *out* in the Navy. Show and Tell! Many a Navy Seal is still trying to plug the gap he left behind . . . Slick Sam the Sailor Man!"

"Christ," Victor mutters during the applause.

Slick Sam the Sailor Man is a gloriously physical specimen. Naturally lanky, unnaturally augmented, his physique is casually, confidently displayed. He fails though, even in his guise as a sailor, to avoid the ratty hair which plagues the go-go profession. The jaunty sailor's pillbox perches on greasy lank tendrils framing heavy features not quite coarse enough to be distinctive.

"A smile would help," Victor says to David. "If it weren't for professional tattoos, he'd look like an ex-con. But hey, Humphrey Bogart managed to be a sex symbol, and he never had a body like that."

"Except as a rental," David snaps.

"Lies." David is just being provocative.

When the navy-blue sailor pants fly off with a practiced flick, it dawns on Victor that tear-away track pants are basically stripper technology. Sailor Sam prances like a fiend during the fast song, peeling with exuberance, as if naturally his clothes prefer littering the stage. During the touching power ballad, he oh-so-slowly, oh-so-coyly shimmies out of a well-worn jockstrap. In the pouch is a velcro pocket for cash and phone numbers. Sailor Sam flips the jockstrap into the crowd, aiming for money like a lucky horseshoe heads for the post.

Naked now except for army boots, white socks, and sailor hat, the go-go dancer's cock dangles crooked and fat. He offers the goods to the front row, the cheap seats, where sly shoppers congregate for deep discount contact.

"Tea bag, tea bag," a fat drunk young man calls out.

The tea bagging ceremony at Buffoons is steeped in tradition. The exquisite ritual is stripped to the essence: dancers squat to dip musky baskets into fevered faces.

"Tea bag, tea bag," the fat drunk young man pleads. Tilting back his head, he sticks out his pointed tongue and waves it from side to side.

"Tea bag! Tea bag!" The crowd takes up the chant.

Sailor Sam saunters towards the fat drunk young man with a wide rolling gait like he has to swing out his legs to walk around his balls. So close, and so three-dimensional you could smell him (Contradiction for Men), Sailor Sam bunches up his cock and balls into a bruised-looking, swollen, and twisted fruit, and works a nipple with his other hand. A ripple of muscle jolts across his body as he flexes, pretending to crank his genitals around another full rotation. The fat drunk young man shudders and falls back into his seat, overcome. He no longer wants the tea bag. The fat drunk young man had paused for an instant at the intersection of celebrity and fantasy, calling out his request, but then shrank away, craving too much of what he could never have.

"That's disgusting," David says, breathlessly watching Sailor Sam twist his nuts into a turkey skin balloon.

"You get what you ask for." Victor's words are drowned by applause.

With a quick slap of his dick from hip to hip, Slick Sam the Sailor Man bounces off the stage.

Looky Loo returns. "So. Do you know what F-A-G really stands for? Fucked up, Antagonistic, Gay people . . . oh wait, I'm supposed to be joking." No one laughs, except one shrieking maniac in the corner, whose shrill bray incites a rippling echo of amusement. The brayer's embarrassed table-mate – like a cat in the litter box, or a driver caught in gridlock – averts his gaze to the middle distance.

"So. Did I tell you I forget to masturbate? I tried putting it on my list of things to do. Buy Groceries. Masturbate. Pay Cable. . . The cable gets paid and I forget to masturbate. *I hate that.* . . . Sure – go ahead and laugh, you wankers." Loo directs his bitterness at a handsome laughing young man in the centre of the room. "You probably already *beat* off today, didn't you? First thing this morning, right? Well – I forgot to do that."

The crowd laughs again.

"Didn't he already tell that joke?" David asks.

"It's not a joke," Victor says.

David looks horrified.

"And now fresh off the farm," Looky Loo announces, "veal on the lam. Here he is: Randy Goose!" Randy scampers out, a slim waif with acne and feathered blond hair. Unbuttons his plaid shirt. Dances to the beat of a different drummer. He stumbles struggling out of his cowboy boots and falls over trying to dance while removing his tight jeans.

"Randy chicken," Victor suggests.

"Farm boy my ass," David declares. "Send him back to the go-go factory."

Primed by the pump and grind of Sailor Man, David's already thinking of the baths. But there's no point getting there too early. He never dreamt it would happen, but yes, he's now officially sick of married men.

Let the breeders finish dribbling out their spunk and go home to wifey. Then bring on the sex pigs.

Sex pigs of the millennium unite! David smirks, enjoying Victor's quizzical glance. *Dyslexic sex pigs untie!* It was always a challenge to escape from Victor at just the right point on the upswing of an evening. He wanted to keep Victor company, but not get dragged down by all the heavy gravity.

Victor too is planning escape. If he hurries he might just catch the end of Clean Freaks, his favourite night at Narcotics Anonymous. *Imagine,* Victor surveys the audience at Buffoons, *the hottest addicts in town all in one room.*

Victor has discussed it with his sponsor but hasn't quite got around to telling David he is in recovery. *The hottest addicts in the city*: Victor did not quite know how to say simple straightforward words like that to David. The whole topic was loaded.

Victor hasn't even told David why the sudden motivation for a lifestyle make-over. The "news" had made an impact, and the importance of things crystallized in different ways. The "grave consequences" were not all as predicted. One new unpredictable element was a need for privacy. Victor started keeping secrets. He started protecting himself, protecting his new, fragile, precious, core – even from David. His sponsor said it was okay, to keep going to meetings and talking, but he didn't have to tell David anything. David had his own issues.

Victor worries that David – given his excesses – would feel judged. So far, Victor has been deflecting booze by saying he needed to diet. It was "the zone." He was cutting out carbs to lose weight.

"Can't argue with that." Later, David would offer him a drink and then remember, "Oh yeah, you're too fat. Sorry." And later still: "C'mon, have a drink for crissakes. You're not that fat!"

In the middle of the night, the phone wakes Victor. It is David, phoning from Starfuck's – on the route of his standard deviation from the baths.

"What's up?"

"Nothing." David sounds quiet and small. He doesn't apologize for waking Victor. Confused and jarred awake, Victor is automatically sympathetic. "Did you get laid?" he asks.

"Kind of."

"What happened?" Victor yawns.

"Well, there was this chemistry major guy. He was hot. But his idea of reciprocation was, like, watching in the mirror while I blew him."

"Yeah."

"Yeah. And there was this leather daddy guy. He seemed okay and fucked me, but started calling me Bruce."

"Bruce."

"'You like that, Bruce? You want my cock up your hungry butt, don't you, Bruce?' All I could think about was, who the hell is Bruce? I was half-hoping Bruce would show up and get this guy off my back."

"Go home, David," Victor says.

"Okay."

"You going home?"

"Yeah." David yawns now too, like he just realized how tired he was.

"Go home."

"Okay."

"Okay. Bye."

Victor places the phone down. He picks it up again and orders a taxi. He's heading over to David's. It amused him, on the odd occasion, to imagine that David needed him. Dressing quickly, he runs downstairs, taking Henry James with him in case he can't get back to sleep. A never-ending story, that's what *The Turn of the Screw* has become. He keeps losing the thread and has to start over.

He wonders in the cab if maybe he was scared to finish the book. Finishing things was not providing much sense of accomplishment. He needs new goals, that much is obvious, but does not want to set himself up for disappointment. It was easy right now to be optimistic in a cab at three in the morning flying through the empty streets. Everything seemed possible. Maybe, he thinks, I'll just go there and tell David everything. He imagines David's weak, whiny protest: Why are you telling me now? – and he could just say, Well, you woke me up, and as far as I'm concerned, now is as good a time as any.

CHRISTMAS IN KATHMANDU

The Big Bell Café offers a great view of monkeys scampering over balconies and rooftops, performing the monkey version of West Side Story – the same jostling gangs, but way more graphic masturbation displays.

Jared wrote this line on postcards to be sent all over. This year was "Christmas in Kathmandu" and he wanted everyone to know it. He sipped ginger tea and dashed off postcards of the Kumari virgin, a deity embodied in the person of a young girl who is heavily made-up, never touches the ground, and replaced when she starts to menstruate.

Sure is different here, Jared wrote. *In Christianity, the virgin is pregnant.*

Perched atop a seemingly vacant building, The Big Bell Café was sheltered, sunny, and overlooked Durbar Square. A large temple bell hung just beyond the chalkboard menu, and the heart of old Kathmandu bustled below: the market, the hippie remnants of Freak Street, firewood vendors at the feet of monumental stone lions, fabulous temples, whirling cascades of pigeons, incense, and diesel fumes, beggars with knobby stumps for hands, sacred cows eating garbage.

The erotic temple, coyly highlighted in all the guidebooks, featured carvings of inconceivable couples: horses, donkeys, dogs – all depicted copulating or with erections. The rafters at the four corners were large wooden men, massive erections one-third their length pointing up their chests. Tourists flocked about, tittering and taking lots of photos.

When Jared first saw the Western woman at the café, he thought, *American*. Too no-nonsense to be anything else. Henna highlights, thirty-something. She glanced at Jared and returned to her companion, a cute Nepali boy, maybe late teens, full-sized like a man, but lean, and pretty. He looked awkward in a new suit. He paid her attention, Jared noticed. Something was going on. This ballsy American had hired a smiling broad shouldered Nepali lad, and he didn't look like he could guide their way out of the café.

The next day the Western woman stopped by Jared's table. "May I?" she asked, pulling out the empty chair. "Please," he said, as she settled in. He flipped his postcard, so the painted Kumari virgin faced up, and henna-ed strumpet with balls faced down.

"I saw you yesterday," he said. "Decided you were American."

"Part-time American. One foot in Montana, one in Alberta."

"You must be very flexible."

She laughed. "I saw you yesterday. Knew you were a big fag."

Jared blinked.

"Gloria." She held out her hand. "Part-time dyke."

Jared smiled and shook her hand. "I missed the dyke part. Your nephew threw off the gaydar."

"My nephew?" She looked puzzled, then burst out laughing as Jared indicated with his hands, about this tall, shoulders out to here. "Oh, you mean my gigolo."

"My, aren't we candid."

"Just between you and me? My pet name for him – The Warm Dildo."

"That's . . . so sweet."

"You think he's something." Gloria leaned back and pointed straight at Jared, narrowing her gaze. "You should get a load of the gigolo's boyfriend." She paused for a moment, then her laughter burst out and rang across the square.

Gloria suggested they all meet the next day. The Big Bell at one. Then she and the gigolo would have to leave. He wanted new shoes, and finding the perfect pair was a challenge.

The gigolo's boyfriend looked like the gigolo's older brother: angular and handsome, but larger, sterner, more self-confident, more full of himself. Jared could see how the gigolo might turn out after his apprenticeship. The boyfriend kept checking his watch, a large shiny "Rolox" which screamed secondhand from a cheesy businessman who bought them cheap.

Boyfriend took the gigolo with him when he left to oversee his pressing affairs.

"He's a bit much, isn't he," Jared muttered, mostly to himself.

"Oh, I don't mind." Gloria slung her arm along the back of an empty chair. "Whatever it takes to keep the dildo warm and charged up."

"But what do they *do*?"

"Can't imagine. And wouldn't dare ask."

"I can't imagine either," Jared exclaimed. "That's the worst part."

They laughed awkwardly, then decided to go smoke hash. "Merry fucking Christmas," Gloria kept saying. "Merry fucking Christmas."

"*Glor – or – hor – horia.*" He draped her in garlands of marigolds. "*Gloria in excess dios.*"

"The ver-ry one," she sang along. "And a merry fucking Christmas to you."

There was something about the boyfriend that intrigued Jared, something beyond his erect posture and severe yet delicately rugged features. The Nepali's fierce, proud masculinity emanated a sort of disdain, like he judged those around him and found them lacking. Jared wanted a piece of this man, wanted him badly, and would pay for it, even if that meant widening the chasm which already separated them. It was Christmas, after all. *I've been good for so long.*

Jared arranged to meet the boyfriend at the Karma Kanteen. Usually in Nepal Jared ate vegetarian, but this was the night before Christmas. He ordered chicken. The boyfriend ordered a grilled cheese.

Boyfriend's English had gaps. He was interested in import-export and life in the West. He clearly thought Jared was lying about homeless and hungry people. He was angry Jared tried to trick him. He'd seen *Dallas* and many American movies. "Do you think I am know

106

RANDOM ACTS OF HATRED

nothing?" he finally burst out, switching and switching his utensils like a shell game.

Jared did not know how to respond. He said, "Food is taking a long time." Boyfriend made a dismissive gesture: "Cheeken" – as if that explained everything.

Boyfriend finished his grilled cheese and smoked a Marlboro before Jared started picking at his meal. Jared's appetite fled as he uncovered slender, compact bones. Dinner became an autopsy. He feared rat. In the lamplight of some night festival, he'd seen fat busy rats patrolling the cold streets like conical cats with pointed heads, short legs, and hairless tails.

He pushed his plate aside and thought about pie. *Really fruity pie.*

Walking back to Jared's hotel and sharing a nightcap of rice liquor, Boyfriend became angry when Jared dared slide his hand up his thigh. "Not touching," he snapped, his eyes flashing. "You not be touching."

No touching? Jared wondered about that. *How are we to do the dance of the sugar plum fairies without touching?*

Boyfriend had his own idea about the piece of himself Jared could buy. The foreigner's U.S. dollars had bought an erection up his ass. Nothing else. No kissing. No tenderness. *A cock up his ass: Not just what he paid for – what he deserves.*

Jared spent Christmas in Kathmandu shitting out cum, squatted over the porcelain hole in the floor toilet, his flip-flops gritty in the treads.

Christmas in Kathmandu

Boyfriend came twice. Both times, the condom broke. It was too dark to tell, but Jared thought the gigolo's boyfriend re-used broken condoms.

"Good lord," he said, out loud. He cradled his head into his arm. The rat rumbled in his guts. "Merry Christmas," he said, the taint of the air rich in his nose, on his tongue, and down his throat, as his bowels emptied with a splash.

"Merry. Fucking. Christmas."

108

THE BIG RED PICTURE

At the memorial service, tension clumped in knots as thick as the sprays of white chrysanthemums dripping from the coffin.

Doug sat surrounded and alone. Dry-eyed, motionless, his back straight.

Peter arrived late and slipped into a pew at the back. He did not permit himself to perceive any ripples of consternation at his presence. There were no glances, no whispers.

"Of course I'm going to her funeral." He had been surprised that Doug assumed he wouldn't. "Do you think I'm not a part of this?"

Doug would not look at him. "It's not something I could ever want you to be a part of."

Peter sighed. "If you don't want me to go, I won't."

"Whatever." Doug shrugged into his jacket. He was going home. "I can't tell anybody what to do."

Doug and Kate had met Peter in Portland. They could never quite remember how the three of them came to share a hotel room after the birthday party. Doug and Kate had planned to rendezvous in Portland with their friend from Olympia, but at the last minute he flew to Hawaii. Peter was driving back from San Francisco and stopped to admire Mount Hood looming rosy amber in the setting sun. Peter made one phone call to a number from a previous trip to San Francisco (where he always seemed to meet other tourists) and stumbled onto news of the party. As luck would have it, Peter's friend did not make it to the party, either. Neither did they meet the Birthday Boy, who remained in high donjon with his inner circle and, rumour had it, was never quite fit for presentation. "Everyone's been turning thirty lately," Peter commented. "These affairs can go either way – celebration or mourning."

They were all from Vancouver, they did have that in common – at least while visiting Portland. Their meeting almost seemed arranged. When Kate and Doug arrived at the party, the first friendly face was Peter's, looking a little lost. Kate made the introductions and confessed to not knowing a soul. "Neither do I," Peter said. "Oh, where you from?" "Oh, my god – so are we!" They clumped together chatting in an outward-looking island, scanning the sea of strangers. Kate made a big deal about coincidences, so it would have been like her to insist, *No, Peter, don't even think of driving anywhere tonight. Stay at our hotel. There's plenty of room, isn't there, Doug? No bother at all, really – I'm menstruating anyway.*

Kate was prone to large, generous gestures.

The hotel room only had one king-sized bed. Kate said they were all just going to pass out anyway, "Unless you boys start talking about dinky toys." She giggled, and Doug looked up and shrugged. As Kate had said, she was the evening's "designated drinker."

As they undressed, Peter noticed how built Doug was, how extremely well constructed, his broad shoulders tapering to tight small waist and hips. Doug was all over red – a freckled carrot-top with permanently flushed skin and golden red furry highlights spread across the autumn foothills of his chest. Lighter wispy red tufts of hair sprouted from his armpits. A web of copper threads, glinting in the light, dusted his limbs. An alluring chestnut trail led down his stomach and disappeared into his underwear. Joe Boxer. Polka-dot smiley faces on a tartan background.

Earlier, Doug had asked if Peter played squash. *Perhaps we could squeeze in a game*, he said, forced to press against Peter as others jostled past. They talked at length at the buffet, the cacophony swirling past them. *Was* Peter's job at the Human Rights Commission really a career move and *did* Doug volunteering at the Food Bank help out more than his time was worth? *I mean, really. In the big picture.*

"Where's Kate?" Peter asked.

"Oh I don't know," Doug said looking around. "Probably making new friends in the bathroom." He sniffed loudly, and burst out laughing like something was really funny.

Peter appreciated Doug asking where he grew up, instead of *Where are you from?* Many who ask where Peter is from reject the answer "Vancouver." The real question is rephrased less delicately: *No, I mean – what are you?*

The Big Red Picture

If it works into the conversation, Peter will mention his Korean grandparents. He just doesn't like to be asked right off the bat, like it mattered somehow, like it would possibly tell something about him.

Well over six feet tall, Peter is large, hearty, and jovial. His presentation contributes to ethnic confusion. Much taller than either of his parents, he towered over his shrinking grandparents. Peter's suburban middle-class childhood was a North American stereotype in many details, the two-car garage, white picket fence, a tricycle in the yard, but tiny Omma and Appa retained the ability to make him feel foreign. Scrubbed for presentation, uncomfortable in his best clothes, he remembers incense, ambiguity, fiery *kim chee*, so much food, and feeling increasingly hollow professing gratitude. Peter felt unseen, yet was being groomed and assessed in relation to the other grandsons.

Peter had sat his parents down and told them he was gay, which they found shocking but irrelevant. Gayness was nothing, a symptom only of being too caught up in the free and easy allure of a selfish lifestyle. It was a phase, like a pleasure-cruise, but not a valid destination. Certainly not a definition, or an identity. He had to see it for what it was and not make so much out of it. He had to realize where he was standing, that's all, and then he would see that this, this thing, this gay hobby, was not really an impediment to marriage. In fact, recent examples from family history show duty being done, a blind eye turned when necessary, and everyone happy. But this gay thing? See how it works. You are young now. It only gets worse. No one is happy.

His youngest sister summarized the prevailing sentiment: "Marriage hides everything, Peter. Much indiscretion may be swept under the rug of matrimony."

The turmoil of adolescence had flung Peter into a complementary orbit with a pale gawky boy who lived down the street, and had freckles and this amazing auburn hair, of a colour and unruliness that Peter had never imagined possible. One day they walked home together from the library and by the next week were best friends. They squealed with laughter at their own cornball humour, not knowing what it meant to camp. Almost twenty years later they continue, in the style of seventies television, to offer sage advice with an Oriental bent: *The lug of matrimony, glasshopper, hides a rot of dirt, but you still notice the rumps.*

Crawling into bed, Kate took the side nearest the bathroom ("just in case"), still talking of the party. "Can you believe that guy running around with the pantyhose on his arms and legs?" She sat cross-legged in a long black T-shirt, brushing her luscious black hair. "And that black velvet woman with the spider hat, who was *she* with?"

Peter slid into bed on the other side. Doug took longer, strutting around in his underwear. *Does he know I'm watching?* Peter wondered.

"Doug?" Kate mumbled. She burrowed under the covers and curled up around her hair brush. "Doug, you're bushed. Come to bed." A languid hand stretched out towards Peter. "Goodnight, uh – ?"

"Peter."

"Goodnight, Peter," she said, satisfied.

"Goodnight, Kate." Peter smiled at her even though her eyes were already closed.

Doug had casually offered to sleep in the middle. A sacrifice of comfort on his part, he implied. The ironic heterosexism amused

Peter. *Number one breeder rule: A guest male must at all times be separated from an attached female.*

Gay is good, gay is great. Peter watched Doug return from the washroom. Doug stretched and yawned, arching his back, the muscles of his limbs and torso garnished with gold, before he turned out the light. *Everything works out perfectly, like at the gym where I shower with the men. No wonder people fret about gays getting special privileges. We have special privileges.*

The love that dare not speak its name was really just a tactic to keep the ranks exclusive. *Dare not speak*, really means, *lest we be swamped and implode from sheer irrelevance.*

Doug climbed into bed over Peter. For a fleeting moment Peter felt the sensual weight of Doug's body. He felt like a large cat – firm, loose, muscular but not tense.

"Sorry," Doug said to Peter, and kissed Kate good night.

Peter doubted he would be able to sleep. The sight of Doug's flesh had stirred him. The danger was he might forget himself and embrace Doug. When Peter had a boyfriend, he really enjoyed sleeping together, cuddled like puppies in a heap. He could easily be all over Doug like a rash, a friendly arm slung around him, a throbbing sleep boner squashed up against the crack of his smiley-faced butt.

Won't be getting much sleep tonight. Tired, delicious, ambiguous regrets.

In the dark, Peter replayed the scene of Doug's casual striptease, his strutting and stretching, yawning in his Joe Boxer's. In bed, Doug's foot stretched out and touched Peter's leg, then retreated. Then it was back, touching, a cold heat. *Is this a signal, a secret connection?* Peter did not move away, his awareness vibrating. Doug's foot stayed in place. Adjusting his position Doug's hand brushed Peter's arm, then was gone. Doug's hand came back, but stopped just before making contact. The heat from Doug's fingers radiated against Peter's hypersensitized skin.

Will I get punched out? Or does he have manners, and I'll only be contemptuously cold-shouldered?

Boldly, heart thumping, Peter reached out and squeezed Doug's fingertip.

Doug moved his hand away – *making a fist?*

The hand returned, a warm weight covering the back of Peter's hand.

YES! *We have contact.*

Neither Doug nor Peter slept much that night. First they waited to ensure Kate was truly asleep. Her chattiness had quickly melted into gentle liquid snores. "Like purring," Doug whispered. "Snorepurrs. SNORRRRRE-PURRRRRR."

With a deliberate, casual thoroughness, the men explored each other's bodies, trying not to giggle or flinch as horny callouses slid over silken skin. Each time Kate moved in her sleep, they froze, the tension mounting, their throbbing erections pulsing with lives of their own, interactive lives they encouraged and which grew and built, a dual spiralling vortex attracting strength and sweetness.

They did not come, no, not that night. Not even once.

Not with her there.

Squash was Doug's cover story. Packing his racket, white court shoes, and workout clothes, he headed off "for a couple of games, with Peter."

They met at Peter's small apartment. Only one article of Doug's

The Big Red Picture

workout clothes was ever put to use – his jockstrap – and squash remained largely theoretical. "Squash balls," Peter mused, "sound like hors d'oeuvres. . . . *Squash balls?* Or what happens" (he pressed into Doug) "when people confuse horseplay and foreplay."

Doug returned home flushed from his workout, eyes gleaming, his damp hair a darker auburn. *Squash is good for his mood*, Kate thought. *Makes him more playful and affectionate.*

In fact, Peter and Doug actually played squash only once.

Doug belonged to the YMCA and had competed in a squash ladder. Stepping into the rectangular white court, Doug became aggressive and intense, unable to accept losing even one game. Peter, playing for fun and losing graciously, performed (in his own words) with "a certain spontaneous *savoir-flare.*"

The small white room, with its echoing squeaks, black marks on the walls, and red boundary lines, seemed to concentrate each personality.

"If I'm in your way," Peter made a point of explaining, "I'd rather you call a let than hit me with a ball. I've had those donut welts on my back and Jesus – do they ever hurt."

"Don't worry," Doug said with a grin. "No one will get hurt."

Doug easily won the first two games. In the third, Peter, relaxed and insouciant, finessed a brilliant series of cross-court shots. Doug, down five-love and caught out of the control zone of the court, frantically rushed forward and slammed the ball out of bounds, above the red line. His swooping exuberant backhand smacked Peter right in the face.

The game was over. Peter's nosebleed garnished his white "Mr Noodle" T-shirt and left round red splotches over the floor of the court, freshening the paint of the crimson base line. Doug rushed to the service desk for an ice pack, which he solicitously applied. "Sorry, buddy," Doug said. "I should've called a let." His prompt action made Peter wonder if Doug had been in this situation before – was wild careless swinging a habit in Doug's game? To suppress the thought, Peter attempted a joke.

"I can just see your backhand advice in a squash manual," Peter said thickly through the compress. "Instructions: Apply racket smartly to face. Repeat as necessary until nose is thoroughly squashed."

Later at home, telling Kate the story of Peter's nosebleed and his brave attempt at humour, Doug made an offhand comment: "That's probably the first and last time we ever play squash – "

He froze. The cascading accuracy of his words echoed in his head.

It was a confession Kate could not miss.

Two days after Kate discovered her husband was having an affair, with a man, Peter was helping Doug collect a few things. Kate left work early, unable to concentrate. She arrived home to find both of them in the apartment, and flew into a rage.

Kate, Doug said gently in the face of her flush anger. *Kate.*

Don't you fucking Kate me, she screamed, grabbing Doug's keys off the counter. *Don't you* FUCKING KATE ME!

Doug had to sell the car, his prized candy-apple red Mustang.

Did she have to do that? Doug wondered. *Did she have to ruin my Mustang?*

Doug loved that car.

The Big Red Picture

No one could explain why Kate didn't just make a scene, milk the drama for all Doug was worth, and write him off. Instead, Kate drove off in the candy-apple red Mustang, jammed a pistol into her mouth, and scattered herself back through the mists of time and meaning.

The car might be cleaned, but it would never be the same. It was sold, directly from the police pound, for a fraction of its value.

And so, despite the shock, life went on – if to go on meant getting up in the morning, because that is what Doug did, even if he had been unable to sleep.

Doug felt guilty but could not talk about it. Kate's screaming indignation echoed throughout his life. *Don't* YOU *fucking Kate me.*

The waves of turmoil dashed the two stunned men up against each other. The same basic facts – a romantic triangle – could be arranged into many different stories. In the social maelstrom, Doug's friends, mostly couples he'd shared with his wife, offered at best awkward condolences. The news of Doug's bisexuality apparently also conveyed the information that he was available. To everyone. Guys hit on him, which he never expected. Married guys. After what had happened, it was exactly the wrong thing. He was used to flirting with the wives, playing his part in a safe charade, but a husband had never before laid a warm hand on his back and then slowly stroked down past the waist – just to see what would happen. Smiling and saying *buddy, fun, play*: all in the same sentence which ran on to judge him uptight, for a bisexual. His hurt pride laughed off, never any harm in two men looking for a romp. No harm in trying.

Doug was flabbergasted. The entire casualness of it Doug found unsettling. After all, he was still in a relationship, and to be hit on so soon. . . . His resentments seethed.

Based on the feedback, he wondered about these guys who claimed to be just like him – bisexual, whatever. The question was, was he just like them?

No one blamed him, to his face, but everything changed. Doug and Kate had worked well together as a couple. Now he reeked of death and the wages of sin. Of course no one ever said that. He wasn't exactly shunned, but neither was he embraced.

In the confusion, Peter remained a reliable, loyal companion. He made himself available, for trips to the gym, or hikes on the North Shore along the Baden-Powell Trail, or quiet times cocooning. They rented movies from Inferno and cuddled on the couch. Inspired by a new level of intimacy, their sex life reached a new plateau, not better exactly, but different, and this seemed like progress. Peter and Doug decided to live together, and moved into a loft tower in Yaletown.

Returning to the building one evening, Peter nodded to other regulars of the elevator rush hour. Peter imagined Doug sprawled on the bed, moping. He caught himself wishing Doug wouldn't be home. He craved a few minutes of peace, alone with himself, un-burdened by *not talking*. The unspoken had taken over, like a black hole, except with Doug, everything was red now. Even the hair in the sink.

Doug was home, and worse, had been rummaging in the closet under the stairs to the sleeping loft. He still had boxes he didn't know what to do with. "Open concept loft living" was just another way of saying, "no in-suite storage." A framed photo of Doug and Kate in fif-ties drag at Jericho Beach with the red Mustang could not be thrown away or displayed: much of these boxes fell in the same category.

The Big Red Picture

Doug pulled out a curvy blue plastic ice pack shaped like a mask.

Peter removed his tie.

Doug turned the blue plastic mask over in his hands. He held the ice mask up to his own face, then flung it back into the box.

Peter did not say a word, hanging on the audacity of the moment.

"You know," Doug said, his voice catching, "she was my best friend and I let her down."

In the coffin, her face had been wrong. She looked serene, but like an imitation, even though her face had not been damaged. The carmine lipstick was a shade she would never have worn, and over-applied, slightly clownish. She looked like somebody Doug had never loved. If Doug allows himself to remember, he shudders as that wax dummy image insinuates back through time, replacing happy memories with interposing events.

"It's okay," Peter murmured, stroking Doug's back. The long supple muscles along the valley of the spine reminded Peter of filet mignon.

"Gonna grab a shower," Doug said.

Peter couldn't tell if this was a rebuke. Since the accident, Peter has held Doug and petted him with sincere warmth and affection, expecting nothing in return, remaining silent so Doug could speak if he chose. Peter was old enough at thirty to be experienced at loss. He tried to give Doug space without seeming distant. Sought to comfort but not smother. Offered continuity while allowing Doug time.

Doug has never cried.

Peter's friends repeatedly warn of the perils of loving a bisexual: Hello! News Flash on the All Gay Channel . . . *Bisexuals are too much trouble! Been there –* DONE *that.*

Peter's childhood friend – still freckled and unruly – speculated that once Doug recovered from the shock of Kate's sudden death, his affair with Peter would also be over; implying an essential sickness at the heart of Peter's relationship with Doug, which Peter resented.

Another friend said, *It's, like, so totally co-dependent. Obviously your little redhead is just using you right now cuz he, like, needs you.*

If that is the case, Peter changed his clothes and straightened the room, *if Doug only needs me until he can recover, well, maybe in the big picture that is not a bad thing.*

Doug returned, moist and glowing ruddy, and threw himself face down on the bed. Naked. *Merely a shower, not a rebuke after all.*

The sight of Doug spread out on the bed, waiting, his back limbs and butt a study in rose, coral, blush, and terra cotta, made Peter think his friends were just jealous. Massaging Doug's back, he worked down to his buttocks. Spreading Doug's legs further apart, Peter arranged Doug's balls and cock so they were displayed, squashed and blood-maroon, at the apex between Doug's thighs. Peter kneaded Doug's buttocks, lightly stroking ticklish hips and flanks. With stronger circular caresses, Peter spread Doug's cheeks, blowing gusts of hot provocation on moist rusty hairs. The liver-coloured pucker winked in anticipation. Their sex life had become, according to Doug, experimental. At first, it had been more back and forth, but now was honed to one practice: Doug getting fucked. It stirred Doug, being the passive object of desire, being touched. To be penetrated did not remind him of her. . . .

The Big Red Picture

She is still with us, here on this bed. Just as she was that first night when she sighed and turned over and we froze. Remember, we froze. My hand froze on your chest. Your hand froze on my cock.

She mumbled something and slipped back into oblivion.

Your sweet lips, still frozen. A face moist from tender, secret kisses. . . .

– Or are those tears at last?

122

RANDOM ACTS OF HATRED

You never know with men. Any man could glimpse flashes of ass and thigh in the ripped black jeans, glance up to Todd's large eyes, his loopy grin, shaved head, and gorgeous skull; hate feeling attracted, hate their impulse to fuck him, hate his knowing disdain, hate their second orgasm, and especially hate when later, they're sucked in all over again.

A surly Newfie skinhead, Todd cruises and services construction workers, fake cops from the Tool Box, leather daddies from the Barn, any man who will let him. Except suits. "You gotta have standards," Todd would say. "Old enough to get an erection, and anyone but suits. Men are bad enough. But suits – can't stand the fuckers."

Todd likes men with hair on their chest and stomach who know what they want.

This man was like the rest of them. They were starting to blur for Todd, one burly aura blending into the next hairy torso. Wearing faded jeans, black leather chaps, and a dirty T-shirt, the man had left the Barn, glared at Todd, hooked his thumbs into his belt, his meaty hands framing his crotch, and invited Todd up to his apartment with a jerk of his head. Closing the door behind them, he ordered Todd to his knees, unbuttoned his fly, and brought out a large handful of meat. "C'mere, punk. Come take care of this." The man's cock approaches horizontal, the crooked knob glistening moistly.

"It's your fucking fault, punk. Your fucking mess. Clean it up. With your tongue."

The hairy balls astride his nose, Todd licks and licks and then sucks the sweet, salty shaft. Todd, on his knees, the cock of a man he hated, hates, hates stretching his lips until cum drools out the corners of his mouth.

Todd spits and wipes off his face. "You came so fucking fast, like it's a fucking race or something." Annoyed, Todd doesn't even bother finish jerking off. Idly stroking his chest, he wonders how long before that cock, a small sticky mess like a hairy dessert, will become hard and demanding again.

Growing up in Come by Chance, Newfoundland, too pretty for a boy, Todd feared those men reeking of fish bait, who followed him into the night, caught him where it was dark, pulled him towards them and forced his face down into their crotch. More than one guy cuffed Todd up side the head for scraping his hard-on getting it out. *Kneeling on gravel in the dark, guiding boners out through flaps and zippers – Christ, it's easier getting dogfish out a gillnet. Couldn't they just unbuckle and drop their drawers? Noooo. That would be too much of a commitment.*

Todd learned to cocksuck years ago, practicing first on his brother Steve, then with his brother's friend Matt, who was cute but brutal, and once with Steve and Matt together, back and forth between them, everyone pretending it was the first time anything like that had ever happened. *Looka the faggot*, Matt said, stroking his own drooling cock. *Looka the cocksucker. His own brother the cocksucker.*

Wants cock so bad. C'mere, you fucking faggot.

Steve and Matt each shot a load in Todd's face, then spat on him in ejaculation replays. They sneered at the cocksucker, punched one another in the chest, and that was that. It never happened again.

Except – just before Steve's wedding. Christ, Todd hated weddings. There's something about getting married that makes guys keen for a blowjob. And they could be pretty pushy about it, especially if they'd been drinking, and who didn't just before tying the knot. Steve wasn't that rough when he was fifteen, sixteen, and only spit on Todd that once with Matt, which was okay – even if he did spit first. Matt was Matt and he had to show off. Matt's lingering need to despise Todd was volatile, insistent, feral, and secret. The best man at Steve's wedding, Matt pulled Todd into a bathroom, unzipped the fly of his rented tux and said, *You don't deserve this, you cocksucker. Not for one fucking minute.*

Steve too was suddenly rough. Just before Steve's wedding Todd learned to deep throat – had to, or else choke to death and Steve wouldn't have noticed. Steve's calloused hands grasped his little brother's head and worked it on his cock, hips jerking, buttocks clenching, eyes closed, face a grimace. Todd hated that Steve went so far away while his cock was down his throat.

Soon after the wedding, Todd shaved his head and left for the big city. There he was fucked with abandon. Fucked by men who desired him for an hour, fucked by men who hated him from the start. Fucked by men who carried a torch and fucked by men who carried self-replicating strings of genetic material.

Todd hated that the big city turned out to be so much like his family.

As a teenager, after practicing with Steve and Matt, Todd went to work for Uncle Fred. Fred lived down the way and used to be married but his wife left. Now he needed help around the place.

Fred paid very little and actually expected yard work – mowing, raking, pruning. "It's hot," Fred said. "Take off your shirt, and I'll grab a couple beer." His uncle's eyes crawling up his back felt like bugs Todd couldn't brush off.

After enough beer, resenting working overtime for no more money, Todd returned his uncle's gaze. Fred, paunchy and moody, sauntered over. "There's work to be done in here," he said, directing the boy into the potting shed. Fred's moustache scratched and his kiss tasted foul – like ashtrays and old beer and something rotten. Todd flinched when his uncle grabbed his ass. To distract him, Todd felt up his uncle's crotch, then squatted down. His uncle's cock was loathsome; sharp piss and whatever it was, that smelly smegma paste like festering locker rooms and curdled cottage cheese. Beer and cigarettes, that's what Uncle Fred was like. Second-hand beer, cigarettes, smegma, and piss.

One day Fred wouldn't let Todd fall to his knees. He held him up, pulled him into a slobbery embrace, and then bent him face down over a shelf for transplants. Pushing one joint of a blunt thumb into Todd's butt, Fred spit repeatedly into his other hand. Removing his thumb, he pressed the head of his prick against Todd's asshole, gripped the boy firmly, and pushed. Todd almost passed out from the pain. He cried while his uncle fucked him. He never hated anyone as much as he did his uncle at that moment. As the summer went by, Todd cried each time his uncle fucked him after yard work, until that scarlet yellow day – it was the fall – he didn't cry, he let go somehow and said *Yes, oh god, yes.*

That was the last time his uncle ever fucked him.

126

ACTING INNOCENT

Though past the time for academic credit, Jeffrey still felt determined to plow through the supplementary reading. Credit, he felt, was entirely personal.

He held R. D. Laing's *The Politics of Experience* in his hands and stared into space. And to his credit, as well, he could confront the direction of his thoughts. He was nursing a distinctly unhealthy distraction and there was no point denying it. There was no point denying anything. He was doomed.

Doomed to be helpless and pathetic. Doomed to be completely unable to stop thinking about – *him*.

He had been in the bathroom a while and Jeffrey had a pretty good idea what he was doing in there. Jeffrey wondered if he ever used the Canadian Tire catalogue, but how to ask such a question? The catalogue fell open to summer scenes, happy little families in inflatable pools. Did any of these models push his secret buttons? A young dad, hairy-chested and work-hardened, yet surprisingly slim, and uncommonly handsome. Or the young mother, cute, bouncy, firmly contained. Larger pools had room for more than one couple. Usually two smiling guys, with a girl between them, the other girl bringing drinks. Two shirtless guys in the same picture was exquisite, even if interrupted by a girl.

Nakedness signals a competition.

Who knew what he could be thinking about. Jeffrey didn't really want to know, but the craving, the not-knowing, lingered in Jeffrey's head like a hungry ghost.

And that ghost hovered, indelibly potent, yet hazy and inexact. He could not see the beginning and he could not see the end. He just knew he was haunted. Haunted by a lust he could not talk about.

His blond hair turbaned and another towel around his waist, Ken wandered down the hall to his brother's bedroom. Jeffrey glanced up from his book. "Hey."

Ken slumped against the door frame. "Does he ever put the moves on you?" he asked, sounding indifferent.

Jeffrey blinked. "Who? Well, yeah. Kinda. What?"

"In the lap pool? He said he could improve my stroke by a good seven inches."

"What did he mean by that?"

"Jesus, I wonder. A seven-inch *stroke*?"

"He was on the swim team." Jeffrey felt obliged to point out the obvious. "That's why his parents got the pool. So he could train at home."

"Yeah, sure, now he's a coach. Like, in the sauna–" Ken settled into a wide-legged stance and lowered his voice, "You know, you look kinda like a young god."

"He said that? A young god?"

"Yeah."

"Which one?"

Ken paused. "He didn't say."

Jeffrey also thought his brother looked like a god. Apollo, as a puppy. A golden lab puppy Apollo draped in a precarious towel. Ken and their sister Suzanne were both emanations of their mother, Liz, fair and radiant, a serene paleness belying turbulent natures. Jeffrey took after their father – dark, thick, and heavy, the value of his solid square attributes bound to appreciate over time. Later, perhaps, he'd appear distinguished. So far he just felt lumpy. Square, and lumpy.

Jeffrey kept his eyes fixed on the page, exercising his discipline to *not look* at the hair trailing up to the bellybutton, *not look* at the towel tucked over one hip. "Just ignore him. That's what I do."

"Should we tell Suz?"

"Nah. He's just playing. You know? Flirting because that's what he thinks we want. Probably thinks it's flattering."

Truth was, Ken was flattered. Gerald was tall and angular, more broad than thick, chest covered in hair, his torso and legs pale, long and lean. Gerald's blue eyes and dark hair provided a contrast far more arresting than blond hair, blue eyes. His sister's blue eyes felt cool and distancing, but with Gerald, the intense connection was turbocharged by Ken's fevered enthusiasm.

Gerald was their sister's husband.

In the sauna, Gerald cupped his crotch like it took both meaty hands to contain it. Gerald was a peacock, Jeffrey said. He didn't spend much time with his brother-in-law, even though they lived in

Acting Innocent

Gerald's house, at least for the summer, longer for Ken, who might not graduate as expected.

Jeffrey had firmly resolved, upon his return from first year college, to "come out" to his brother. Despite near-panic anxiety, he did manage to blurt out the truth.

Jeffrey was dumbstruck – almost angry – when his brother languidly brushed the revelation aside. "Yes, of course. We both are." That they were both gay Jeffrey had never considered, but Ken, younger and in many ways swifter, had been waiting for his brother to clue in. *Jeffrey was really smart, sure – but boy, was he dense.*

The brothers had a bond with a new dimension, and in a new way too, Jeffrey found Ken's physical presence disturbing. As a matter of principle, Jeffrey never liked blonds, sharing with his dad (before they stopped speaking) all the familiar prejudices and an arsenal of dumb blond jokes. *Why did the blonds cross the road? – They couldn't remember.*

But now Jeffrey was dealing with a whole new challenge.

Seventeen, blond, and glowing: that was Ken. Jeffrey was not much older, and as solemn as a young child, one not yet self-conscious about being sincere. Ken was in heat; Jeffrey had been stewing in his own juices for two years longer. Ken, faster and flirty, cranked up the pressure. That's why this fruitless obsession was tearing Jeffrey apart. Everything was always a joke for Ken. What does Ken really mean, and what was just the way he was? When people are just being themselves, it doesn't mean anything.

And Jeffrey wondered what was just the way *he* was. Depressed, maybe. Scared. Perhaps he was just like a teenager. He was after all nineteen.

RANDOM ACTS OF HATRED

And the little monkey had become the biggest flirt.

Jeffrey felt seized by the certainty that only he knew how incredibly right something was meant to be, with only one little detail to clear up.

The one little detail had a name. It was called incest.

Is it so bad, he wondered. *The traditional taboo prevents inbreeding. Okay. But surely it's not meant to apply where procreation is impossible. Surely the very nature of an incest taboo is homophobic.*

The new brothers never talked about incest, or taboos, or if the fruit of their loins could ever condone a mutual embrace. What happened instead was madness. United in a vision of glorious liberating defiance, they decided to come out to their parents.

The announcement one groggy Saturday morning that both their sons were gay came as a rude shock to Burt and Liz. That day dragged like a bad hangover. At seventeen and nineteen, how did the boys even know? Unwavering, the boys insisted they did know. Like a catechism from a cult they chanted: *I did not choose this. I did not choose to be born this way.* It was the boys' stubbornness, their lack of diplomatic flexibility, that got them thrown out.

"There's always a choice." Their father, livid, slammed the door behind them.

"Jesus H Christ." Burt slumped into his chair, the bluster gone out of him. "The name is going to die, Liz. Our name is being flushed right down the toilet. We are being shot straight to hell. Thank god my parents are not around for this. They slaved for this. For nothing. All our work, all our day in, day out – it's all come to nothing." He reached for the remote and turned on the game, any game, raising the volume, eyebrows clenched down tight, eyes fixed on the screen.

Liz retreated to the kitchen.

Acting Innocent

Liz lied to her sister Barb to cover up the shame: like a throw flung in the air to hide a messy bed.

Not both boys, Liz convinced herself, *both boys can't really be that way.* So it was not really lying. Liz said the boys had been caught doing drugs right in the house. Barb was shocked. "Needles!" she shrieked. "I don't believe it. Jeff and Kenny always seemed like nice boys." Barb gloated a moment about their sullied perfection, then was seized with anxiety about her own brood, whose promise had never been clear. *Maybe it's for the best they don't go away to college, if they come back drug addicts. At least – mine aren't on drugs.*

Barb's eldest, Carla, was a sensible girl, if a bit pig-headed. Never one to dress right, but old beyond her years, and knew how to handle her brother Peter. A good mixture of sternness and tolerance, Carla talked about becoming a cop, even though that was no life for a woman. If only Peter had half her sense. Peter was born with a nose for trouble and so fond of wheels – his life was downhill and fast. Since that mix-up with the borrowed cars, he's been in jail. Just as well. At least he's safe in there, locked up away from the drugs and bad company.

When Peter gets out, Jesus, Barb hated to think what could happen. She spread ashtrays around the yard even though people were incapable of using them outdoors, preferring to flick their vile butts right into her tractor tire flowerbeds. *Pigs. Every last one of them.* She laid out the butt-cans like shrines of hope, each large tomato juice can weighted with sand and full of empty promise.

For their annual barbecue, Barb and Carl more or less went whole hog. One year they even hired a band – their daughter Carla was dating that guitar player, and enthusiasm over that turn of events swept over into believing the boyfriend's band would be a good idea.

"Burnt Lemon" didn't go over well. Apparently, irony is an acquired taste. Burnt Lemon was deemed loud, lame, raucous, and worst of all, stopped playing too early. The next year Barb and Carl went right back to liquoring up the familiar talents. As predictable as they were, they were popular, and there's something to be said for that. People don't bitch if they don't have any expectations. Sometimes it's better not even to try, if you're just going to get shot down.

Barb scanned the sky, worried about the clouds lacing the horizon. The weather forecast covered all the bases; sunny, hot, chance of thunderstorms. A thunderstorm would clear the air but ruin the evening. Jeffrey and Ken – what if they showed up? Liz said not to believe anything they said. It broke her heart to say it, but they'd changed, you couldn't trust them anymore. *You just can't. Don't let them out of your sight. You don't want to know what they're doing.*

Barb didn't know what to make of it all.

When the boys were thrown out by their parents, and taken in by Suzanne and her husband, the young couple risked being branded as traitors. Suzanne said she didn't care, but they all knew better. They still didn't know if Mom and Dad were going to the barbecue.

"Caught between a rock and a hard place." Gerald repeated her words to Ken in the sauna. Hair dusted Ken's tanned limbs with glints of gold. Gerald absently stroked across his own chest with a veined hand, a wave of damp curls springing back up glistening with the sheen of a nighttime pond. "Your sister said, she felt like she was caught between a rock and a hard place."

"She should just forget them." Ken was suddenly angry. "Forget them. They're just a couple of old people to say goodbye to."

Acting Innocent

Gerald had been generous, insisting the boys make themselves comfortable in the large house he'd inherited along with his father's construction company. He complained about the property tax but enjoyed welcoming his wife's brothers into their spacious home. Gerald thrived amid the jostling orbit of male satellites. He found it a challenge, though, to deal with the obvious puppy love. Just a phase they were going through. A rehearsal. Not really about him as much as it was about them being teenagers. He tried to remain steady, to be a mentor for the boys. They would never be men among men unless an adult stood by them.

Some couples start with a dog, Gerald teased the boys. *Look at us. A golden lab would've been great. We get a couple teenagers. We'll never want kids after this.*

The large house had seemed empty with just him and Suzanne knocking about from freezer to microwave, from work to bed, without even servants requiring them to keep up a front. He wouldn't go so far as to call the puppy love "hero worship." It wasn't that, but still it touched him, even though he knew it was nothing. A phase. At times he felt distracted, scared even. The boys mattered to him. They mattered. Suzanne and the boys were his family, and their father was being an outrageous prick. Suzanne was smack in the middle and she was not one to give an inch in any direction. Couldn't say too much to her or her dad.

Gerald felt nostalgic for his own teenage impulses: courting temptation, acting responsible and feeling the whole time like doing something reckless and wild.

Without getting caught.

Taylor Contracting Ltd was Gerald's dad's company. Started after the war, and grew steadily, in spurts, with a lot of work, which seemed natural for a construction company. Then Gerald's parents both died in one of the bad pile-ups on the highway. Holiday weekend, everyone in a hurry, the fog rolls in and people don't even have enough sense to slow down. Gerald's dad had braked to a crawl, emergency lights blinking, when they were rammed from behind. First by a van, then by a loaded tractor trailer. Rescue crews threw up separating the wreckage, pulling out the bits of flesh left on the charred carcass.

Gerald came home from college for the double closed-casket funeral and never went back.

At the time, Suzanne was working lunches at Potter's Diner and Gerald starting seeing her there. He lived alone in that big house without even a housekeeper. Five days a week he ate at the diner. Suzanne's shift, Mrs Potter had pointed out. *So you're here are you*, Mrs Potter had mentioned, *'Spect the Taylor boy will be in*. Suzanne suddenly realized what everyone else had already noticed – that Gerald Taylor only came into Potter's because of her. She felt herself go hot, embarrassed for being the last to catch on.

When Gerald did show up, right on schedule, her question sounded like a challenge: "What do you do when I'm not here?"

"Miss you," he said quickly, then flushed up from his collar, the thrust of his body finally reaching his head. His face reddened. Neither Gerald or Suzanne could speak, awkwardness cocooning them in its symbiotic embrace. Later, when she refilled his coffee without meeting his eyes, he whispered, "Movie?" and she flicked her eyes to him and just as quietly said, "Yes."

Gerald took over Taylor Contracting as executor of his father's estate, intending to keep up the contracts and sell the business as a going concern. The jobs went well, sympathy levels ran high, work kept coming, and it never seemed right to sell.

Gerald made an effort to be popular with the crew. The older guys who remembered Mr Taylor said the boy didn't come up short, no matter how much the new guys grumbled. A bunch of lazy pricks who never worked a day in their lives, that's what the new guys were. Gerald worked alongside the men, pitching in with whatever needed done, even hard and dirty work. Cold two-fours appeared on hot Friday afternoons, especially if it looked like they'd be working late. But not only then. In front of the crew, Gerald would talk back to the foreman and that always got a laugh. In private, Gerald combed through budgets with each project foreman, and said: "This one, I know, it's a challenge, I know, but I'm giving it to you for a reason."

Suzanne was flat on her back, napping on the couch. She had to close her eyes a second or else she'd never make it through the barbecue. *Wake me at four*, she'd said, sounding so exhausted.

Gerald hunkered down on the carpet and started stroking Suzanne. He caressed her arms and legs and belly.

Ken watched from the doorway, then approached the couch near his sister's head. He knelt down, squatting on his heels. It was mesmerizing, watching Gerald.

So tender.

Ken knew that Gerald knew. He often watched Gerald, probing into his privacy, as if he alone could unlock the mysteries of manhood. Like it all boiled down to private mannerisms. He watched

Gerald's thick-veined hands slide up Suzanne's thigh, shoulder muscles bunched under his t-shirt. The soft thin cotton emphasized his strength. Gerald could look more virile and imposing in a t-shirt and jeans than other men do in uniform. Ken's cock twitched, and he spread his knees wider.

Suzanne arched cat-like into Gerald's light touch. She turned on her side and sighed, sounding determined to go on napping. Her face was smooshed into the cushion.

Gerald stretched out on the floor next to the couch. He sprawled on the carpet on his back and his head came to rest on Ken's thigh.

Gerald settled in to become more comfortable and his head rolled against Ken's cock, which inched out another pulse in response.

Ken was thrilled but horrified. What if Suzanne opened her eyes?

The great length of Gerald was spread on the floor for Ken to survey. The loose folds at the crotch of Gerald's jeans held an ambiguous promise. Gerald's hands rested on his belly and his eyes were closed, like he too had decided to settle down for a nap, and naturally Ken's thigh was the pillow.

Ken's erection struggled next to Gerald's ear, pinned by the weight of Gerald's head on Ken's baggy shorts.

Suzanne stirred on the couch, and opened her eyes. "Oh my god." She sat up, her features blurred. "What time is it? I told you to wake me."

Gerald did not move. Ken's thoughts flashed in a panic. *We'll look guilty if we move*, he thought. *If we're innocent we'll just act innocent.*

Suzanne padded out of the room. Gerald stood up quickly,

Acting Innocent

paused for a second to tousle Ken's hair – Ken flinched as from a blow – then followed Suzanne out of the room.

"Jeffrey and I finished making the potato salad," Gerald called out after her.

"Good," she yelled back.

Adjusting the chrome-framed wings of the vanity mirror over the bathroom sink, Ken's cock twitched hard before he even touched it. *Hand-made porn.* He grinned watching the triple reflection of a smooth young blond guy masturbating. Using the mirror was way more exciting than just looking down at himself, past his skinny chest and flat stomach, the thin golden hairs darkening as they trailed from belly button to the boner thrusting from his tidy bush. He pouted, frowned, then tried looking shocked, shy, coy.

Turning from side to side, he watched himself caught and starting to shudder: blue blue eyes, dark stubble highlighting his jaw, faded jeans riding low on the hips, bulging wet crotch, the liquid twitch of muscles along the spine like snakes wrestling, his back, his back, *his.*

Gerald laid on the horn. He sat in the driveway in their faded blue-grey Volvo, all the windows rolled down. Jeffrey in back, Suzanne in front cradling two ice cream containers of potato salad.

"What's he doing in there?" Suzanne said. "Get this thing going and crank up the air con, honey. My tits are melting."

"It's only five minutes."

"Could be a pleasant five minutes."

"Won't even be cool by the time we get there. And you'll only be spoiled. Only makes it worse."

"Wouldn't mind being spoiled just a little bit." Suzanne sighed.

"Maybe you'll be spoiled later?" Suzanne greeted Gerald's slight leer with a mild disgust. "Maybe you'll have gone bad?" She ignored his nudge.

Ken was taking forever to get ready. He appeared briefly on the doorstep, looking hurried and languid, then ducked back to turn down the central air conditioning. Ken locked the door and slid in the back next to his brother.

"Finally," Jeffrey said.

Ken's wet hair stuck out oddly. This disarray was achieved in an inspired frenzy after coming to with his forehead pressed to the cold mirror, eyes closed, a mess on his hands and several other unlikely locations. In combination, the bathroom and a veneer of vanity was a teenager's best friend.

"Cold showers are never usually so long," Gerald said, stepping on the gas. Air defeated by the heat whipped through the windows.

"What were you doing?" Suzanne asked, her tone dramatically *I could care less*.

"My hair, this weather – what can I say?" Ken looked over and spoke to the depth of his brother's eyes. "Just trying to *keep cool*."

Jeffrey smirked.

"I can't believe we're going somewhere away from the air conditioning," Suzanne said.

"It's your family," Gerald said pointedly. Ken and Jeffrey looked away from each other. PMS was no joke, and if they laughed, Pretty Moody Suzanne would let them have it.

Suzanne sighed again. "Mom and Dad will be there." She said it

Acting Innocent

confidently, like *Time Heals All Wounds*. No one spoke. "This better not be too weird." Now she sounded doubtful.

Sticky questions hung in the air. The car felt like a drafty lurching sauna with unfortunate plastic seats. The four of them fidgeted, each movement sliming flesh. The looming family barbecue blotted out the horizon.

Jeffrey recalled his cousin's brief phone call. News, Carla crowed, news that can't wait.

Carla picked him up in her battered patched Pinto and they drove out to the basalt bluffs. He scowled at the joint she offered.

"Do you know why you got kicked out?" Carla squinted against the smoke.

"No fags in the house?"

"You wanna know?" Carla exhaled a great cloud. "What your mother told my mother?"

"Jesus, Carla, how do ya keep a fruit in suspense. Spit it out already."

Carla laughed. "Well. You'll be as shocked as I was."

"What?"

"Drugs!"

"What!"

"Shooting up, right in the house." Carla inhaled the nub down to the last cherry burst, rubbed it out like snapping her fingers and swallowed the roach with a swig from the shapely Coca-Cola bottle she had nestled between her thighs. "I'm disappointed in you, Jeffrey. Where are your manners? You didn't even offer to share."

When Liz had come by with the news, Barb could see she was upset. Liz's hands flew in circles from her elbows like propellers unable to fire up. Liz usually aimed for a cool poise, but nothing fooled Barb. Liz being so frankly upset was convincing. And Barb was worried too, of course, because Carla had maybe been acting a little strange. Remote. It's normal for a girl to have secrets, but what does Carla have to hide? It's not like she's dating.

Barb was scrubbing inside the cupboards after Liz's visit, which made Carla uneasy as soon as she came into the kitchen. Much about cleaning eluded Carla, especially any need to clean what you can't see. Tradition, Carla felt, did not make itself right just by being tradition. Especially female tradition, if it involved cleaning behind the fridge.

Carla did not hear female tradition calling her name.

So much about her mother seemed unnecessary to Carla. Barb held herself down. She deliberately made herself look smaller, and helpless, unable even to walk in those ridiculous heels, tottering like an infant, and with that same small helpless infant's concentrated power. The need for protection gave the man an opening: he stumbled in and took over without seeing the trap. To Carla, the whole charade seemed pointless. It was far easier just to walk upright on her own without advertising for a crutch.

Her mother was looking at her strangely.

"How are you, dear?"

"Fine Mom."

"You know, dear."

"Yeah."

"If there was anything wrong, you could tell me."

"Yah-ah?" Carla acted nonchalant.

Acting Innocent

"You would tell me?"

"Of course, Mom."

"So you seen the boys?"

Carla drank half a glass of water. "Went over to the house yesterday."

"How they getting on over there?"

"Fine."

"Dear – you know why Burt and Liz asked them to leave?"

Heartbeat. Heartbeat.

"Can't imagine," Carla said.

"Well – what did the boys tell you?"

Carla knew her cousins had been kicked out for making such a big Broadway musical song and dance production about *being gay*. But what could she say? *What did the boys tell her?* She shrugged. "Not much."

"They musta told you something, dear."

"Just that, you know, Burt's a prick. Breathing down their necks. They're boys, they need some freedom. Christ – they're teenagers, Mom."

Barb knew she hadn't really been answered but her daughter was a woman of few words, most of them coarse. Suddenly Barb's fears felt foolish. There was no need to worry about Carla, who had always been a very no-nonsense kind of girl.

"Well, of course the boys are not bragging about it. It's nothing to be proud of."

"What isn't?"

"Well, dear," Barb said, "I'm sorry to tell you, but Jeff and Ken are on drugs."

"Drugs!" Carla sounded surprised.

"Needles, Liz said."

"Don't believe it."

"You've seen no signs then?" her mother asked, relief creeping into her voice.

"No." Carla said with conviction. "No I have not." She concentrated on *not laughing*. It was too funny. Jeffrey was such a goody two-shoes he wouldn't even toke up with her. And Ken was way too prissy to touch a needle – unless he was sewing.

"I knew there was no need to worry about you." Barb gave each of the cabinet doors another little circular swipe. "You've always been sensible."

Wait until I tell Jeffrey, Carla had thought, spinning the tale in her mind. Enjoying this moment with her mother because it was a gold mine of rich, absurd details to be shared later with others.

"Oh my god!" Aunt Barb shrieked at the sight of them walking up the driveway. "You made it!" Her delight was to the scale of crossing the Rockies on foot, instead of driving across town and parking down the street.

She hugged each of them with loud enthusiasm. First Gerald. Then Suzanne. Then Gerald again, a tight squeeze, her head at his chest, her breasts flattening into his stomach. "Oh, I mean it. Thanks for coming."

Jeffrey and Ken both stared at the ridges where Gerald's T-shirt clung to his torso. Hints of flesh are more compelling than absolute nakedness. Ken's eyes flicked back to Gerald's chest, hair slowly writhing like tent caterpillars under the thin wet cotton.

Gerald tugged the T-shirt away from his moist skin.

Acting Innocent

Aunt Barb moved on to Jeffrey and Ken. "Just look at you. And you. A sight for sore eyes. You must be breaking the girls' hearts. Where are they? Your girlfriends? Good-looking guys like you."

"Mom and Dad?" Suzanne asked.

Aunt Barb's smile faltered. "In the house."

Gerald and Suzanne exchanged glances. So did Jeffrey and Ken. Aunt Barb started spluttering. "Three barbecues. Three in the backyard. All in the backyard. Are you hungry? The buffet on the patio. The barbecues at the back. The booze is – can I get you a drink? What would you like to drink? Carl's dying to see you. Carl's out back. Beer, Gerald. Would you like a beer?"

Another round of glances and gender lines were drawn. Suzanne went into the house with Aunt Barb to take care of the potato salad. The three guys headed back to the firepit, joining the masculine orbit around Uncle Carl. Gerald got along with Carl better than the nephews did. There was something about the nephews Carl did not quite understand. He considered them overeducated, although only Jeffrey remotely qualified, with high school and one year of college. Carl was put off by even the expectation of higher education.

But Gerald was alright: he had been smart enough to give up school and do what he had to do. Living up to duty plus making money at it was a glorious combination. Money was the measure of a man's worth, Carl thought – as long as he did not have too much of it. Too much money only made people ridiculous. Worse almost than having no money at all.

Carl's nephews – he did not know what to make of them. His alarm bells went off, he knew something was wrong, even if he couldn't put his finger on it. They got along with his daughter Carla, that's for sure, got along like a house on fire. Something was going on, and they thought they were pulling the wool over his eyes, he knew it. He didn't trust those two boys, not when they were young and not now. They never answered straight. Either they were looking down at you, or everything was some big joke they couldn't bother explaining because you wouldn't get it anyway.

If he was their parents, he'd have kicked them out long ago, no questions asked.

Too big for their britches, that's what Uncle Carl thought. He shook Gerald's hand and offered him a beer out of the cooler.

Then he shook hands with his nephews and offered them beer. He didn't even bother to joke about them being too young to drink. He just gave them each a beer.

And felt as awkward as hell.

Carla came out of the house with a case of beer to stock up her dad's cooler. In this heat, out there with three barbecues.

"Who's winning?" Carl asked, face beaded with sweat.

"Not the Expos."

"Fuck a duck," Carl said. "Excuse my French. What's the damage?"

"Not a hope in hell."

"Fuck, encore." Carl liked the Expos just because the Montreal Canadiens had been such winners. "Gimme a beer, sunshine. I need to drown my sorrows."

"Hey, you guys," Carla said to Ken and Jeffrey.

"Hey," Jeffrey said. Ken took another drink. His beer was practically empty, while Jeffrey's was almost still full.

"It's so weird, you know." Carla nodded towards her father

busy checking the coals. One barbecue was "his," one was mostly for corn, and the third was the "open" barbecue – for control freaks who had their own special way of doing things. "Freaking weird. In the house, he's helpless. Couldn't boil water to save his life. Never hear the end of it if he had to lift a finger. But outside, over a fire, wind him up and watch him go. Christ, men are so primitive they could be the missing link."

"Missing Link Discovered At Family Barbecue," Ken announced.

"Men may appear to be an evolutionary throwback," Jeffrey agreed, "but really they're a clever means of preserving vital skills. When civilization collapses, men like your father will save the day because they will know how to cook meat over a fire."

"When civilization collapses," Carla said, "he still won't ever have lifted a finger in the house."

"Like – you do," Ken said to Carla.

"That's different. He won't because he's a man."

"Well, that's what Mom is for, isn't it?" Ken sounded ironically cheerful.

"To Mom." They clinked bottles.

"I was reading about this thing," Jeffrey whispered. "You know that gay cancer thing? They're saying it might be like the flu or something. You know? People spread it."

"The flu?" Ken asked.

"Gay cancer is contagious?" Carla whispered. "What's the gay part in gay cancer?"

"Sex?"

"What?"

"Means you might prevent it."

"Preventing gay cancer," Ken said.

"Jesus. Stay away from boys – cuts out all kinds of trouble!" Carla hooted at her answer.

She is such a dyke, Ken thought. If she's not a dyke she could be without even half trying. Does she know, he wondered. She was never petite. Never girly. Stereotypes, sure, but hello – she lives in jeans and watches sports with her dad. Everybody's just waiting for her to come out. She wants to be a cop, wants to wear a uniform and be one of the guys and have everybody know that there is nothing wrong with her.

Carla gave Ken another beer. "Cheers, bud," she said, clinking their necks. The cool beer slid down quickly.

"You're a dyke, aren't you," Ken said, quietly.

Carla stared at him, frozen.

"I mean, no shit, Sherlock. No one will bother to act surprised."

"You're disgusting." She loudly stated this as fact, and walked away.

"What?" Ken turned to Jeffrey. "I mean, if it walks like a duck and quacks like a duck. . . ."

"Some people." Jeffrey looked over his brother's shoulder around the backyard. "Some people just don't wanna know."

Barb checked the hotdog buns defrosting in the microwave. "It's a brave thing you've done, dear. Taking in the boys. Be careful not to get involved."

Suzanne paused with the melon-baller. "I am involved." She was making a special dessert. Melon and Grand Marnier, choice of vanilla or chocolate ice cream. Something light and fresh. Just for "the girls."

"Of course you are. I mean with what the boys are doing. And Gerald too. Keep an eye on Gerald. Wasn't that long ago he had a bit of a reputation. Before he married you, dear."

"Gerald?" An edge crept into Suzanne's voice. She scraped at the cantaloupe half. "There's no problem with Gerald, Barb."

"Oh no, dear. It's just stuff like this spreads. People get started innocent enough, might be fun, why not give it a try. Before they know it they're hooked."

"Believe me, I should know. Gerry's not like that at all."

"No, no, of course not, dear."

Ken planned to use the toilet just inside the back door but it was occupied.

He headed upstairs and ran into a clot of relatives in the hall outside the kitchen. Aunt Marsha. His mother. Great Aunt Hazel and her daughter Nancy, who was at least forty but never left her mother's side. When Nancy was a girl, Hazel was told to put her in a home, and as she has ceaselessly reported ever since, she replied from a very high horse: "She *is* in a home."

Ken could see his father with the guys sitting around the living room, watching the game.

His mother looked away from him and Aunt Barb moved in between.

"Even rabbits eat their young," Ken said, but then thought about chipmunks, aw-shucks cute but fiercely anti-social: chipmunks all kick out their children at the same time each year, then stand around screaming, *No, no, not here, go away, anywhere but here.*

His mother looked up. "It's not our fault." Liz sounded hurt that he would dare suggest otherwise. "You made your father kick you out. We love you, but by god, there's a limit to what we can put up with."

"So much BS." Ken shuffled his feet. "I have to go to the bathroom." He sniffled loudly. Allergies. He really suffered this time of year.

The women totally overreacted. He'd only said BS. Even *bullshit* was not half as filthy as their potty mouths.

"I really have to go. Excuse me." He tried to brush past. Barb reached out to hug him tight. "Ken, why are you breaking our hearts?"

"Look, I really have to see a man about a dog."

"Let him go," his mother said.

No one moved.

"Jesus H Christ," Ken exploded. "I'll whip it out right here and piss all over the fucking place. I'll piss on the all of ya!"

People shrank back. Ken pressed through and sprinted up the stairs to the washroom, holding, holding it in at the base of his being until he fumbled opened the fly and let go a torrent into the bowl. A knot inside him also released. The way people moved away, like they knew he was armed and dangerous, that was totally awesome. All he had to do was threaten to wave his wiener around, and people backed off like he was holding dynamite.

He held his cock in his hand and felt the power of who he could be, holding the force of a stream of piss steady, like a fireman braced for a high pressure assignment.

In the mirror he composed himself. Calm. Confident. Indifferent.

"I better go check up on Ken." Jeffrey was worried. Carla grunted and hooked her thumbs into the belt loops of her cut-offs. Her mood had seriously soured. Jeffrey would have to take Ken aside and make him see somehow it was not fair to toy with Carla.

Ken drank too fast and became reckless. He would say anything and think it was funny. Jeffrey knew he could not keep apologizing for his brother.

Jeffrey arrived at the clot of relatives in the hall only to meet his father heading out to see how Carl was holding up.

His father flushed darker. "Didn't expect to see you. Or your brother."

"Now, Burt." Barb moved closer to Jeffrey. "It's not your house. The boys are always welcome here. I'm sure they'll grow out of their little problem."

Burt didn't raise his voice, but he spoke with a particular emphasis. His fury was most clearly articulated by its need to be strictly contained. "Well, according to Mr Know-it-all and his dumb-ass brother, they're never going to grow out of it. They don't wanna grow out of it."

Jeffrey had to say it. "It's not a problem."

"Oh, you poor dear." Barb touched Jeffrey's shoulder. "Please, please know that it is never too late to put all this behind you."

"I can't change what I am. The problem is you guys."

His father was already headed out the door.

"Liz, you talk to him." Marsha sounded desperate. "Maybe you can reach him." Nancy mimicked, "Reach him, reach him."

His mother spoke slowly, measuring her words. "If only you could do the right thing while you're still healthy. If you keep going on like this, you'll only make yourself sick. Eventually. Or worse."

RANDOM ACTS OF HATRED

"Or worse," Nancy burst out with cheerful exuberance, like she had just had the happy thought. "Worse!"

Jeffrey felt overwhelmed: their severe judgment was disproportionate to his exceedingly modest experience. Besides jerking off with Ted Paterson when they were thirteen, fourteen, not even once reaching out across the arm's length which separated them, not ever taking that curious object of attraction, another boy's penis, into his hand; other than that there was just one fumbling encounter with Sheila Nigel where Jeffrey exploded and melted just trying to slip into a condom. "Let's not even talk about it," she said emphatically, which implied she considered him unworthy now even for social intercourse. Sheila Nigel then started going steady with Ted Paterson. Ted's oblique, speculative interest in the girl had been what attracted Jeffrey in the first place. Exploring inch by inch the terrain of Ted's obsession was the closest Jeff ever felt to Ted. *Do you think she always wears underwear? Do you think a girl like that would ever go down on you? Gross. Some guy's cock in your mouth. How can chicks do that? Bet it feels good, some babe.* They beat off together standing up, fists pumping, semen arcing in fleeting trajectories which never intersected. Whenever Jeff saw Ted, even as he had the most fun of his life, even while giddy with excitement, Jeff knew he would cry about this later, as soon as he was alone. Cry about how Ted was unreachable. Even as they shyly, deliberately, began masturbating, the sadness circled closer, and would need to come out later. He liked a boy and the boy liked a girl and the girl liked Jeffrey, the sensitive boy with verbal skills. There was an elaborate game of bait and switch and the girl was the only one to switch. She switched to Ted. So the boy got the girl and the sensitive boy with verbal skills had intricate memories. Memories of fantasies. And he had derived a sort of martyr's satisfaction from bringing the couple together, seeing both pieces and how they needed to fit. The connection was made like throwing a switch. Once united, Sheila and Ted closed ranks and squeezed Jeff out, even though he had arranged to go to the same school as Ted. His shuttle diplomacy was no longer required, becoming in effect a goodbye present no one acknowledged. Jeffrey was just a phase in Ted's life, and the girl was just a phase in Jeff's life. Nobody was in a phase anymore: the surfaces presented were impermeable. Jeff was gay and the other two were engaged, and that was that.

To think that was the most sex Jeffrey ever had – other than the vague compelling intensity of wet dreams, the wetness the reality, the sex but a memory of a dream. Wrestling with the dark blond shadow, kissing him so melting and beautiful and pressing up against him all surrounded and mingling – and woke just as the clear pounding purity of the dream condensed into an ejaculation which for several pulsing moments streamed out in a dissemination of startling intensity. How to explain a wet dream where he slipped into his parents' wedding photos and made love to his mother, younger than he ever knew her, pleasantly boisterous, an athletic bundle of energy who became strong, blond, and male.

How to explain his hazy notions of sex, the details of which he had yet to embrace? How to explain any of this to Aunt Barb, Aunt Marsha, Great Aunt Hazel and her great idiot daughter?

How to explain his desires to his mother?

"Where's Ken?" he asked, brightly.

The knot of relatives twitched.

"You stay here," Marsha said.

"What?"

"He's in the bathroom, dear." Barb took his arm. "And if he's doing in there what he better not be doing, he's abusing" – she groped for the word – "he's abusing, our hospitality."

"What do you think he's doing?"

"Doing." Nancy sounded happy. "Doing. Doing."

"You know, dear. Your problem. You shoulda seen the state he was in. Almost had a fit. You could tell he was desperate. He's changed."

"My problem?"

A crying shame to see it, Barb thought. *Doped to the gills. Always was so smart. Now the poor boy can't understand a thing.*

Jeffrey went into the toilet by the back door. Women called this the powder room.

Jeffrey looked at himself in the mirror, and smirked.

And burst out laughing, choking with laughter, bent over the powder room sink. It was incredible that this had gone so far. Was everyone really so gullible?

Outside, the grown child Nancy started to sway from the tension, her contorted features exaggerating the concern surrounding her. "Oh no," she said. "Oh no."

"Are you okay dear?" Barb called to Jeffrey through the bathroom door.

"Of course," Jeffrey called out.

"We're worried what's going on in there."

Jeffrey threw open the door. "What's going on? I'm shooting up smack. What do you think?"

Shock, horror, even a gasp. Nancy started chewing the hem of her sundress (Hazel would snatch it from her mouth when she noticed) and whimpering, on the verge of tears. Jeffrey felt sad and flippant. Jokes were jokes, but he never meant to be mean. He was already on his parents' shit list, and felt like he had nothing to lose, but still, he didn't want to be mean.

"Just kidding," he said. "Never touch the stuff."

Beer hissed their last as Carl eased open a couple cold ones.

"Sure is," Gerald agreed. "A hot one, no doubt about it."

"Gerald, I have to ask you."

"Ask me what?"

"How do you put up with it?"

"What?"

"What they're doing in the house."

Gerald glanced at the house, then back at Carl. "What are they doing?"

"For chissakes, Gerry, I mean your house." Carl bellied forward half a step and cocked his head. "How can you put up with, you know, what Burt and Liz kicked them out for?"

"Oh, the boys."

"Yeah, the boys."

"Well, Carl, that's not really a problem. Who they gonna do it with?"

"What do you mean, who they gonna do it with?" The certainty of Carl's position was based on everything being outrageously obvious. "They got each other, don't they? Who else do they need?"

Gerald paused. *With each other.* He hadn't thought of that. He'd told the boys not to bring guys home for sex. My home is your home, he said, and I trust you to show respect. If you have a friend, invite him for dinner. Your sister and I want to meet him.

RANDOM ACTS OF HATRED

He never imagined that Jeffrey and Ken would . . . they're gay, that must be what it means. What it really means. They're brothers, but more than that, they're gay.

"Oh, I don't think so." Gerald sounded pretty sure. "I'd know if something like that was going on."

"It makes me feel sick even talking about it. What makes guys get into that shit?"

"I dunno, Carl, but it's their business. They got their own lives to live."

"Tell me, tell me, Gerald, you don't think those boys are sick."

"Young people these days have open minds, Carl."

"Bastard."

Over Carl's shoulder, Gerald saw Burt veering across the lawn as if bucking a strong headwind. "Yeah, it's been so fucking hot," Gerald said, signalling Burt's unsteady approach with a squint and a tilt of the chin. "Burt! Did you bring beer?"

"Who's winning?" Carl called out.

"I don't know," Burt said carefully. "Carl, I hate to leave so soon, but Liz, you know, is keen."

"Well, talk some sense into her."

"Christ, might as well talk sense into a rock. You know how she gets."

"Is she okay?" Gerald asked.

Burt turned and fixed Gerald in the flickering current of his burning glare. "Oh yeah. She's just great. She's having the time of her life."

"You know," Carl said, rummaging in the cooler, his belly resting on his knees. "I was sure there's a beer or two in here somewhere."

Acting Innocent

"It's too serious to kid about," Aunt Barb said to Jeffrey. "You think, you and your brother both think it's one big joke, but it's not. It's very serious and you need help."

"I'm happy the way I am." Jeffrey giggled.

"But you can't live the rest of your life that way."

"I am the way I am."

"But you'll die young. You're always reading about it in the paper. It breaks my heart. We're only thinking of you: I'm afraid you'll have a hard desperate life."

"Wouldn't be so hard if you'd get off my case. I'm gay and that's it. End of story."

"What?"

"You're gay?"

"Gay?"

"Who's gay?" Ken asked, emerging relieved and refreshed. Ken and Jeffrey could not keep straight faces.

"Where's Mom?" Jeffrey asked.

"She went to get your father. They wanted to leave."

"What did she tell you?" Jeffrey asked. "Why did they kick us out?"

"Dear – you're not on drugs?"

"No, of course not. But Ken is."

"That's not funny," Barb said. "Don't even joke about it."

Suzanne put a hand to her heart and her face lit up. "So that's what you were talking about." With her other hand she clutched Aunt Barb with a renewed warmth.

"Yes dear. I'm sorry. Apparently, I was confused."

"I gotta tell Gerald."

"Dear." Barb laid her hand on Suzanne's arm as she turned to go. "It's probably best if your uncle doesn't find out. Carl –" She paused to consider her words. "Carl wouldn't want to know. The drugs was bad enough. This – something like this would kill him."

Barb and Suzanne looked at each other a long moment.

"Okay," Suzanne said, then turned to find her husband. The musicians were still in the drinking stage, booze greasing the skids towards launching a performance of frenetic calm.

Scattered clumps of people were back-lit by a perimeter of citronella candles. Ruby fireflies arced through the humid night air as cigarettes traced out narrative flourishes.

"Ger-ald," she called out above the chatter, her words melting into the haze. "Ger-ry!"

Her husband turned towards her, reached out his arms and said, "Hey, gorgeous. Where you been all my life?" Suzanne giggled and slid her hand up under his T-shirt, and then flushed, remembering what she was not to tell. She turned to find Uncle Carl staring right at her, scratching his belly, a queer, pained expression fighting the smile on his face.

TALISMEN

Under the strobe light, the flashing glow, pulsing neon green, catches my eye. The glowing object is framed by a tattered plaid vest and backed by the smooth parallel perfection of delineated pecs – altogether a splendid strip of torso. In a burst of black lights, the object flares phosphorescent, becoming almost completely luminous.

"Look," I say, nudging the guy next to me. "That guy over there – he's wearing a phosphorescent pacifier."

He doesn't respond, so I nudge him again and shout louder. "He's wearing a phosphorescent pacifier."

The guy next to me is handsome and totally aware of the value of good looks. Faded jeans, filled white T-shirt, an Egyptian medallion on a leather thong. A sentence all in adjectives. The handsome guy glances at me and, unimpressed, pretends my nudging was an accident of overcrowding, pretends my words were drowned out by the bedlam. He turns away to follow a tall guy dressed in faded jeans, sculpted white T-shirt, and an Aztec medallion.

I turn back to observe the punk/skinhead/fashion statement

with the pacifier. Except for the serious and sturdy boots which are totally his own, he is composed entirely of remnants and fragments: one imagines slices from the knees of his torn black jeans safety-pinned across the ass of a friend; in return, material for his vest is torn from the chests of young punk buddies, exposing their nipples. The tattered plaid vest, carefully concocted from these soft-smelling scraps of old cotton, is designed with an acute sense of vanity, not at all uncommon in this setting, but all the more touching in this handsome case. The vest both conceals and exhibits the torso, displaying a careful awareness of what is so artfully presented.

Yes – it must be said (I forge on, the courageous observer), *What a torso*, a torso blessed by a gym membership and discipline . . . or rather, quickly amending my romantic vision, hundreds of push-ups and sit-ups with his buddy in the privacy of their own squat: like Robert DeNiro, only cuter, in *Taxi Driver And Mate*. A torso blessed by crackerjack genes and rampant hormones – a testament to testosterone. Glancing from his broad boots to his broad shoulders, I figure he is a combination of many influences; hormones, genetics, exercise and, of course, packaging.

Framed by the softness of the vest, nestled in the clean sharp cleavage of that torso, that splendid torso, is the item, that talisman – the fetish which first caught by eye.

Neon green, the pacifier hangs from a thick chain, thicker than the chain I use to lock my bike. Keeping the pacifier company, lit by the strobe but unaffected by the black light, is a thinner chain with a crucifix (upside down, of course) and a black leather thong with a silver swastika. I cannot tell in this pulsing light whether the swastika is the original or the turned-around version – the Nazi miscarriage of the original Sanskrit good-luck symbol. It's probably reversible.

Three or four preppy boys noisily approach, bumping through the crowd. Drunk and exuberant and at the same time profoundly shy, they are the kind of totally insecure prep boys who grow up in small isolated towns up north or out west or back east.

The preppy boys spot the skinhead and, amazed and somewhat in awe, cluster around him, as if suddenly confronted by an alien in a zoo. They stand swaying, trying to focus, before reaching out their hands in fascination. The particular object of their attention is, of course, the talisman, the phosphorescent pacifier. The drunkest boy, dark-haired and slightly taller, bends his head suddenly and puts the pacifier in his mouth, making baby-like sucking movements with his jaw. The thick chain hangs from his mouth and drapes around the punk's neck. The prep boys convulse with laughter. The punk remains impassive, accustomed to the attention garnered by freaks. The drunkest boy joins his friends in laughter, and the pacifier flies from his mouth, glistening, and falls back into place on the skinhead's chest, where a line of sweat tentatively explores the sternum.

The prep boys examine all the punk's adornments, fondling the accoutrements like window shoppers; they heft the weight of the thick chain and joke about snow tires, examine the swastika and say *Heil Hitler*, touch with just their fingertips the anarchist pins holding the vest together, and point at the dangling, multi-studded earrings, so unlike the single chaste gold hoops worn back home by boys considered daring.

They touch and hover, they laugh and look; they run the soft worn fabric of the vest between their fingers; they brush against warm hard flesh.

Information spills from the boys and overflows onto their neighbours – they have a need to explain, to tell their stories, to let us know the magnitude of this event. They are used to being friendly. They are used to being able to talk to anyone. These drunken prep boys are from Sudbury. Tonight is the drunkest prep boy's birthday, and the first time he has ever been in a gay bar, but not his last time, they all laugh.

I turn to the guy next to me. In jeans and a simple tight white T-shirt, he sports a voluptuous gym-body which needs no further adornment. Less is more if there's more to show. I lean over his chest and shout into his face. "It is truly a fetish, that phosphorescent pacifier – do you see the way they treat it? Of course" – I shout louder over the music – "I mean, what fetish used to mean before the meaning became worn from rough and careless handling. . . ."

The gym-body gives me a generous view of the tapering v-line of his back and demonstrates the agility of his muscular, protuberant buttocks as he insinuates, haltingly, away through the crowd.

Looking around, I realize there is no one else in this room the preppy boys would have – could have – approached and fawned over so freely as they did the punk boy with the shaved head, chains, and shit-kicking boots. His costume invites, and he receives, as though expected, the attention becoming to an icon – or indeed, an iconoclast.

I silently refuse a beer thrust in my face by a drunken preppy boy from a small northern town.

The prep boys continue standing near the punk, chugging their beers. The punk has accepted a beer (his first tonight) from the birthday boy, and when he looks away the birthday boy looks at him. The punk shifts his weight and his torso dances with his skin.

Yet their energies are so different. The punk calm, impassive, but fueled by a passionate rejection of conformity and yet, I assume, his passions are well-modulated by humour. The birthday boy, the drunkest prep boy from an isolated northern town, staggers among his friends, laughing, one of a pack, nervous, his shyness demonstrated by his lack of inhibitions.

I fumble in my pockets for a scrap of paper and a pen to write something down. (Later, about to do laundry and going through the pockets of smoke-stinky clothes, I discover this scrap of paper and find it makes little – well, frankly, no sense: "climbing the hills of shyness, fueled by beer . . . the obstacle of shyness overcome by beer, only to reach the pinnacle where, dizzy from freedom, shyness turns into its polar opposite and the momentum of lost inhibitions greases the steep slope of the descent.")

The preppy boys, en masse, have to go to the bathroom. I am sure one of them makes the joke about "only renting beer." They all laugh loudly.

The birthday boy, dispensing beers as baksheesh, charms his way through the line at the urinals. He returns first and alone. No longer crouching down with the pack, he is slightly taller than the punk, and slightly younger, slightly slimmer, with fine, sharply drawn features.

"Let's get out of here," says the punk, his first words.

They butt in line for their coats. No one complains. It is, by and large, a very polite city.

Their coats are both leather. The punk's is black, cut in straight lines and garnished over the back and shoulders with chrome studs clustered in patterns like iron filings over a magnet. The birthday boy's is blue, a team jacket decorated with badges and cloth numbers, like a boy scout-cum-athlete. A good jacket will tell a careful reader the whole story of a boy's life to date.

"You need a new coat," says the punk.

"I'm nineteen today," says the birthday boy, swaying, as he struggles into his jacket.

They walk through the cold. After a few minutes, the birthday boy pulls on the punk's arm and says, "Hey, where are we going?"

"To bed," says the punk.

"Where?" asks the boy, as if he hadn't heard.

"Home," says the punk.

They walk through the cold. Snow that had fallen earlier, now dirty and churned by city feet, crunches under their boots.

"I have to go to the bathroom," says the boy.

They walk through the cold.

"I really have to piss," says the boy.

"Well," says the punk with a sweeping gesture indicating the street, city, planet. "There's your toilet."

"Okay," says the boy. He leads them around a corner. "Here's a good bathroom," he says, approaching a fairly clean snowdrift along a line of alley sumac. He fumbles at his fly and pees into the bank, large loopy letters, spelling out the syllables as long as he lasts before tweaking out the last few letters. "Al . . . ex . . . aa . . . nn . . . duh." He shakes himself off. "The great," he says, scrunching over slightly to return his penis to a warm crevice safe from frostbite.

The punk boy steps up to the snowbank. He too writes in the snow. The prep boy, the middle-class white boy from a small northern town, reads it aloud. "F . . . u, fuck, you. Fuck you," he shouts.

RANDOM ACTS OF HATRED

"*Fuck you!*" His words sail off into the city, bouncing off a building or two before being absorbed by the cold and the snow.

The punk finishes the final 'U' and bores a steaming hole deep into the drift. "Low rent beer," he says.

The punk boy lives in a small apartment in a downtown building of a certain age. It is dark. That it is black, in candlelight, does not seem to matter. The punk boy turns up the heat and unzips his jacket. His torso is again exhibited, the sharp cleavage and rippling abs doubly framed by the jacket and the soft worn vest, and the prep boy, looking more often at the exposed flesh than anything else, does not notice a change in the light at the depth of the punk's eyes, or else, noticing the difference, admires them, clear and glittering in the candlelight. The boy's mind is running over. The punk's torso was the kind flaunted by jock boys in high school, the boys he could never imagine being friends with, the boys who were always friends with boys just like themselves, jock boys who did not talk much and found it strange that he could.

The punk brings two glasses of water. "Take off your jacket," he says. The boy does.

"Drink this," he says, handing him one of the glasses. The boy does.

"Do you have any beer?" the boy asks.

"Maybe."

"Take off your jacket," the boy says.

They look at each other for a minute. Then, at the same moment, they smile.

"Take off your shirt," the punk says.

"I need a beer," the boy says.

"Take off your shirt," the punk says, "and I'll see."

Talismen

He smiles at the birthday boy, nineteen today, and goes to the fridge. As he turns away, the boy watches, fascinated by the punk's ears, one of which is unbelievably cute and jaunty, the one with only three or four earrings, a nibbly jewel in the setting of a shaved head.

The punk returns with a beer, rubbing it against his bare abdomen. The boy has pulled his long-sleeved striped preppy shirt out of his jeans, but is suddenly shy.

The punk offers the beer. The boy reaches out to take it but the punk pulls it back and moves his leg forward, so that the boy's hand touches his thigh. The boy jerks his hand back as if burned. They look at each other and then laugh. The punk offers the beer again. "Both hands," he says gruffly.

The boy reaches out with both hands, slowly.

"Close your eyes," the punk says.

The boy does.

The punk moves forward and with his free hand reaches behind the boy, grasps the bottom of his shirt, and pulls it up over the boy's head. The boy shivers as the cool air strikes his torso. The punk touches the beer bottle to the boy's exposed ribs near the nipple and the boy jerks away, laughing, and struggles out of his shirt, throwing it aside. He reaches for the punk but the punk takes a step backwards, and then hands him the beer before moving away. The boy takes a drink and leans back in the chair. His flesh is white and healthy, the torso lean and trim and exquisitely shaped by the benevolence of youth – there is not as yet any sign of the corruption which will envelop him with age.

The punk sits down across the room. The boy takes another drink. "Take off your jacket," he whispers hoarsely, his voice cracking.

The punk slips his hand inside his jacket and touches himself, rubbing his stomach and chest. His knees move suddenly wider apart and then come back, as if his testicles had suddenly become larger.

"Maybe," he says.

The candles flicker, and they are each observed watching the other. After a time, the punk stands up. The boy watches him. The punk puts on a tape, keeping the volume low. They will need to talk in whispers. The music is rhythmic and tribal, traditional yet completely contemporary.

"What's that?" says the boy.

"Dead Can Dance," says the punk, turning from the stereo and slipping off his jacket. He steps over to the boy and stands in front of him. The boy takes a long drink of beer and then reaches out with the bottle, touching the punk with the bottle at the patched crotch of his black jeans. The punk reaches out and pinches the boy's nipple, and the boy pulls away.

"Take off your clothes," says the punk.

"Maybe," says the boy.

"Stand up," says the punk.

The boy stands up in front of the punk. The punk takes the beer out of the boy's hand and drinks from the bottle, finishing it. He throws the beer bottle into the chair and turns to the boy. He puts his arms around him. He kisses the boy on the side of his soft firm neck, at the border between smooth and scratchy, his hands kneading the warm smoothness of his muscular back. The boy, groaning, returns the embrace, putting his hands up underneath the tattered vest and, instinctively, turns to kiss him.

They kiss.

Talismen

This is the birthday boy's first real kiss. Of course there have been others – whiskery aunts, the back of his hand for practice, girls primly thanking him good night: that sort of thing. He only dated good girls. He did not know that not everyone found the rituals of proms and dating so meaningless. He just did what everyone else was doing, especially if it involved drinking.

His experiences with other adolescent boys, his friends, did not permit kissing. Such intimacy was reserved for lovers – unthinkable between boys, even (perhaps especially) between boys having sex.

The birthday boy and the punk kiss and they neck. They neck and hug and grope and growl. The boy is intoxicated by the smells and textures, thrilled by the rough shadow of unshaven skin which extends from the crown to the chin and trails down to the neck, giving way abruptly to satin smoothness which spreads in all directions, the smell of the worn, soft, tattered cotton, many times washed . . . the boy moves away, overcome, and does not resist as the punk unbuckles the boy's jeans and jerks them down over his hips.

"Now take them off," the punk says, going to the fridge. The boy stumbles stepping out of his jeans, laughing, and falls to the floor. He struggles, continuing to laugh, out of his jeans and underwear.

The punk returns with a beer and looks at the boy laying on the floor looking at him. The boy has a hard-on which lays on his lean hip. The boy, now not laughing, licks his lips.

The punk takes off his vest and throws it on the face of the boy who stopped laughing on the floor. As the boy removes the tattered cotton vest from his face, the punk kneels down next to the boy and then straddles his chest, sitting on his stomach. The boy groans and giggles, the punk's weight real but not arduous, and runs his hands

RANDOM ACTS OF HATRED

and the vest up and down the thighs of the punk wearing chains and earrings and sitting on top of him.

Taking a big swig of beer, the punk leans forward and pins the boy's hands on the floor over the boy's head. The punk lets some beer dribble from his mouth onto the boy's face. The boy opens his mouth, moving his head around to try and catch the beer. The punk boy keeps moving slightly so the boy has to move too. The punk sits up to take another mouthful of beer and, looking at the boy, swallows it. He belches. The boy reaches up and strokes the torso which reminds him of so many untouchables in high school and so many unreachables in dreams. The punk, taking another mouthful of beer, leans forward over the boy again, hugging the boy's naked delineated ribs with his black jean knees. The boy opens his mouth expectantly and strokes the punk boy, feeling the smoothness of the skin and the latent vigour of the torso, savouring the softness of the hard muscles, feeling the textured hardness of the thighs under the patched black jeans. The boy moves his head from side to side to catch the stream of pale beer dribbling into his mouth.

The punk kisses the open expectant mouth, sharing the remnants of the mouthful of beer. Stopping in mid-kiss, the boy agape, the punk boy moves away and his throng of fetishes dangle over the boy's face. The boy sits up straining, pressing his lean hard torso into the punk's groin. He takes the pacifier into his mouth, sucking it, eyes closed, hands moving blindly and intuitively over the other boy. The punk sits up straight and the soother pops out of the boy's mouth. The boy's hands move to the studded belt, trying to undo it, and stroke the groin of the black jeans.

"Soother," says the boy, remembering a word.

Talismen

"Phosphorescent pacifier," says the punk, standing up to take off his jeans.

"Pee Pee," says the boy, starting to giggle. "Pee Pee," he says again laughing, gasping, choking, laughing out of control.

The boy, nineteen today, laying on the floor in the apartment of a skinhead in the big city, draws his knees up and slowly stops laughing, becoming calm again and expectant. "Pee Pee," he says, his face relaxing.

170

ACKNOWLEDGMENTS

The following stories have appeared elsewhere:

"The Relative Bargain" in *Contra/Diction: New Queer Male Fiction*, edited by Brett Josef Grubisic (Arsenal Pulp Press, 1998).

"When Parrots Bark" in *The Fed Anthology: Brand New Fiction and Poetry from the Federation of BC Writers*, edited by Susan Musgrave (Anvil Press, 2003).

"The Boy Who Stopped" in *Sights Unseen: Winners of the Third Annual BC Alternative Writing and Design Contest* (Ripple Effect Press, 2003).

"The Brochure" in *The Church-Wellesley Review*, and upcoming in *Donors and Dads*, edited by James C. Johnstone (Harrington Park Press).

"The Boy Who Wore Leotards," "The Boy Who Loved Bugs," and "The Boy Who Sang When Wet," under the title "Against Nature" in *Prairie Fire*.

"Christmas in Kathmandu" in *Xtra! West*, as winner of the 1999 Christmas fiction contest.

"Random Acts of Hatred" in *Quickies 2: Short Short Fiction on Gay Male Desire*, edited by James C. Johnstone (Arsenal Pulp Press, 1999).

"Talismen" in *Queeries: An Anthology of Gay Male Prose*, edited by Dennis Denisoff (Arsenal Pulp Press, 1993).

I would like to thank the gentle folk at Arsenal for ten years of encouragement. I am also grateful to the editors I have worked with: Dennis Denisoff, Brett Josef Grubisic, James Johnstone, Robert Gray, and Susan Musgrave.

Many people contributed to this collection. To name a few of the most persistently helpful: Nathan Pedersen, Sean Eliuk, Brian Lam, and Michael V. Smith. Special thanks to Paula Sten for taking the author photo before there was even an author, and to Anita Levin for helping me to see.

I also wish to acknowledge the generous support of the Canada Council for the Arts.